Bobby and J.R. faced off once more. At times like this it was as if they were total strangers. Brotherly love was never their strong suit. They were driven by a passion greater than love or money. Reaching out for Bobby, Pam was startled by his resolute coolness and detachment. Would his anger toward J.R. make him no better than the man he so disdained?

———————

Series Story Editor **Mary Ann Cooper** is America's foremost soap opera expert. She writes the nationally syndicated column *Speaking of Soaps,* is a major contributor to soap opera magazines and has appeared on numerous radio and television talk shows.

Writers **Paul Mantell** and **Avery Hart** are the authors of plays, children's records, educational cassettes, and humor articles. They live in New York City but have come to think of Dallas as their second home.

Dear Friend,

One of the nicest things about serving as Story Editor for Soaps & Serials books is the opportunity to read the wonderful letters I receive from our readers. It's gratifying to know how much you enjoy these books. At Pioneer we work with the finest romance authors and editors to produce books that recapture, relish, and relive the rich history of soap operas through the retelling of stories that have entertained millions of viewers over the years.

These books bring back precious memories of the past, but they raise questions, too. A reader recently wrote in to ask if Ray Krebbs ever had an affair with Lucy Ewing on DALLAS. The truth is that Lucy and Ray were a hot item in the early days of DALLAS. Their romantic relationship has been downplayed since writers decided to make Ray Jock Ewing's illegitimate son, therefore making Ray Lucy's uncle.

For Soaps & Serials Books,

Mary Ann Cooper

Mary Ann Cooper

P.S. If you missed previous volumes of Soaps & Serials books and can't find them in your local book source, please see the order form inserted in this book.

DALLAS™

7
HOSTAGE HEART

From the television series created by David Jacobs

PIONEER COMMUNICATIONS NETWORK, INC.

Hostage Heart

From the television series DALLAS™ created by David
Jacobs. This book is based on scripts written by Arthur Bernard
Lewis and Camille Marchetta.

DALLAS™ paperback novels are published and
distributed by Pioneer Communications Network, Inc.

SOAPS & SERIALS™ is a trademark of Pioneer
Communications Network, Inc.

ISBN: 0-916217-87-6

Printed in Canada

10 9 8 7 6 5 4 3 2 1

HOSTAGE HEART

Chapter One

It was too early in the morning for problems like this, J.R. Ewing thought to himself as he looked across his oak desk at the two angry faces staring down at him. After the kind of night he had spent with the redheaded beauty he'd met at the Cattleman's Club, J.R. would have preferred to begin the day at a slow and easy pace. Redheaded women don't give a man much opportunity for a long night's sleep, J.R. thought and chuckled to himself, and Judy Whatever-her-last-name-was had certainly been true to her kind.

But those faces looking down at him were not part of a bad dream. Jeb Ames and Willie Joe Garr, his two associates on the Panhandle operation, were indeed standing in his office, flaring at the nostrils and threatening to take their marbles and go home! Early or not, J.R. had to deal with the situation.

Striking oil in the Panhandle section of the state, that dry, northern wilderness, was vitally important to J.R.'s long-term game plan for Ewing Oil. Since his father's retirement, J.R. had run the company, and his goal was to make it the largest independent oil company in the state of Texas. For that he needed the Panhandle.

The Panhandle deal was potentially a hundred-million-dollar winner, and so it carried far more risk than other, smaller deals. Always thinking, J.R. had arranged for other people to face all that glorious risk while he himself had taken none. Those other people, in this particular case, happened to be Jeb Ames and Willie Joe Garr of the firm Ames and Garr. They had the perfect partnership, J.R. thought: He pulled on the strings and they jumped.

But the real surprise to J.R. had come six months into the deal, when Ames and Garr had figured out what was really going on. J.R. had underestimated them for the first time.

"Jeb! Willie Joe! For land's sake, will you just calm down! Now there's no reason for you boys to be jumping out of your skin. I've told you over and over, everything is going to be fine. There's just nothing to worry about!"

But Ames and Garr looked unconvinced.

"Listen, J.R.," Jeb began to complain angrily, "it's easy for you to sit up here in your deluxe Ewing Oil offices and tell us not to worry! But we may go bankrupt on this deal you got us into! And maybe Ewing Oil can afford to lose in the millions, but Willie Joe and I certainly can't!"

"Yeah!" Garr added. "Do you realize how much it costs to drill eleven holes? Eleven!

Eleven, J.R.! 'Cause that's how many we drilled out there in the Panhandle! And every one of 'em has come up drier than a mummy!"

"Yeah!" Jeb chimed in as if on cue, his voice shaking with anger. "And the only reason we're drilling up there in that godforsaken place is on your say-so, J.R.! You swore up and down that we would hit oil! That's why we agreed to capitalize the whole deal and take Ewing in for a third. But now we're losing our shirts! Our company is going right down the tubes—thanks to you—while you sit here telling us not to worry!"

J.R. swiveled his chair around and, with a look of intense concentration on his face, gazed down at the city below him. From his office he could see practically as far as Fort Worth. And nearer, the city of Dallas was like a cat curled up sleeping at his feet.

As annoying as Ames and Garr were being, J.R. thought as his eyes took in the city below, somehow he had to calm these two idiots down and convince them not to pull out of the deal. He had a hunch about the Panhandle, a very strong hunch, and he was on fire to see if he was right.

"Jeb. Willie. Let's be reasonable now," he said almost gently as he swiveled back around to them. "Every geological ever drawn up on that land points to a salt dome field! You boys just need a little patience, that's all! I told you you were getting into a big one. And we're going to strike. We're going to strike big, too! You can count on it! And you know I never steered you wrong before."

Jeb and Willie Joe had pained expressions on their faces. Everything J.R. was saying might be true. And it certainly was true that J.R. had never misled them before. In fact, J.R. seemed to have a sixth sense when it came to oil. If the Panhandle did hit, Jeb Ames and Willie Joe Garr would be two of the richest men in the Lone Star State.

And yet, yesterday, standing out in the hot sun and being told the eleventh well was dry had given Jeb Ames something close to a revelation. J.R. had gotten them into this deal at no risk to himself by giving all the risk to them! And the best he would do for them now was to sit in the comfort of his office and do some smooth talking while their company was out in the field taking the blows.

"J.R., we've had good deals in the past, and we've all made a lot of money," Jeb agreed. "But look at it our way—we're floating this whole project with our capital. One or two more dry holes and Ames and Garr will be nothing more than a Texas memory in the annals of Texas independents!"

Willie Joe jumped in with a plea in his voice. "He's right, J.R. Our company could go bust on this one. We're not exaggerating about that!"

J.R. smiled and tried his best to look hurt. "Aren't you boys forgetting something? Did you forget our little guarantee?" he asked paternally. "Your investment is fully protected by my oil reserves right on Southfork. And, boys, there's enough oil under there to keep Ames and Garr well capitalized until the tenth millennium."

Ames stood up with a sudden, almost violent motion. Slamming his fist onto J.R.'s hard, wood desk, he shouted, "Well, dammit it all, J.R.! Why the hell aren't we drilling on Southfork instead of fedooseling around the goddam Panhandle? The hell with the tenth millennium! We need some return *now!*"

"He's right, J.R.!" Willie echoed.

"Boys! Boys!" J.R. responded with the frustration of a mother hen. "I told you to calm down! Now you know the score as well as I do! When my daddy had his heart attack, I met you right outside the hospital to show you the Red File. You saw his will and you saw the clause he added to it, giving me the exclusive rights to Section Forty of Southfork. If the Panhandle deal weren't to work, you'd get your investment back in spades when the land reverted to me. Southfork has a sea of oil under it—and the way I look at it, that oil would be yours as well as mine, since you're fronting all the money on the Panhandle deal."

Willie Joe Garr looked at his partner expectantly. The promise was good enough for him. And besides, everything J.R. was saying was true. He had shown them the file, he would get the rights to the land and he did agree to share the profits with Ames and Garr if the Panhandle fell through.

But Jeb Ames was not soothed. He couldn't help smelling a rat when he looked into J.R.'s too-sincere eyes. The time had come to put the cards on the table.

"Look, J.R. How do we know that this so-called 'sea of oil' really exists? All the information we have on the Southfork land is from your say-so. For all we know, there ain't enough oil under Southfork Forty to fill up a jar of petroleum jelly!"

J.R. looked from one man to the other, his face full of innocent indignation.

"But I showed you everything on that land!" he protested, his studied patience wearing thin. "Everything! You saw the same reports I did! All of them! Even showing you Daddy's will—do you think that was easy—sneaking the damned thing out of Harv Smithfield's office just so you two could take a look? And you sat right in this office and looked at the geologicals on the Panhandle not too long ago! I mean, fellas, what will it take to convince you? Would an advance on your share help to keep the drilling going? 'Cause if that's what you want—"

Jeb Ames was still steaming under the collar. In his opinion, they were in so deep, even an advance wouldn't do much good. And last week, when he had tried to reach J.R. about an advance, J.R.'s secretary had kept telling him Mr. Ewing wasn't even in. A bold-faced lie, and Jeb knew it from the discomfort in her voice. What he needed now, Jeb thought, was some real confidence in the arrangement. And J.R.'s yammering about a guarantee wasn't reassuring him!

"Listen, J.R. You're not dealing with two farmers who haven't been around the corral. We've had enough talk, and what it boils down to is this—Ames and Garr won't walk from this deal on two conditions—one, you give us that little advance . . . and not too little, either. Two—I want to send my own men in to estimate the size of the hit under Southfork Forty. Nothing personal, J.R., but you're not God. And the way we're going we may be drilling that Panhandle till kingdom come. Now, I checked the estimate on file with the state and I was told the last estimate was made in 1934 when your daddy first got married. And as far as I can tell, that record is too old for me to bank on. Your daddy capped that well in '35, and just maybe he capped it because it was dry!"

J.R. leaned across the desk and smiled warmly. This part would be easy. "I explained once, but I guess you need to hear it again. And you can corroborate this story with whomever you want. Jeb," he continued slowly and clearly, and with a hint of a smile, "my daddy capped that well because my mama's daddy refused to let him drill. My granddaddy was a rancher. Didn't want to see the earth torn up, he said. A clapboard house and a bunch of bovines were enough for him, I guess."

All three men chuckled slightly at J.R.'s little joke, and the tension between them began to ease slightly. But J.R. wasn't home free. When a man like Jeb Ames loses fifteen million dollars in a week by chasing somebody else's hunch, he wants to get his hands on some cold, hard facts.

"Well, I still want to bring my men out or we can call the deal off, J.R.," Jeb said firmly, as his partner squirmed in his chair, astounded that Jeb would talk so gruffly to J.R. Ewing, golden boy of Dallas.

But J.R. was unruffled by the request. "Well, that's fine with me, Jeb," he said almost sweetly, before his voice took on a threatening tone. "But you just make sure that you leave that land untouched. Tell your men to be real careful with my mama's Southfork. She doesn't know anything about the rights going to me after her death. That's just a little secret between my daddy and me and Harv Smithfield, and I don't want her to find out about it now. She's sentimental about the land, and I don't want to see her upset. You understand?"

"Don't worry, J.R.," Jeb said gruffly. "We'll be careful. Come on, Willie." And with that, the two men picked up their jackets and headed to the door.

When they were gone, J.R. turned his chair again to the view of Dallas beneath him and contemplated the situation, the two small lines on his forehead more pronounced than usual. If his mama or daddy ever found out he had promised a piece of Southfork to Ames and Garr for drilling, all hell would break loose at home. Jock Ewing's will clearly stated that no one, no Ewing heir, could ever drill on Southfork. That was the way Grandpa Southworth had wanted it, that was the way his mother, Miss Ellie, wanted it and that was the way Jock himself had come to want it.

What J.R. had shown Ames and Garr at the time of Jock Ewing's heart attack had been a forgery, plain and simple. And, it had worked like a charm till now.

J.R. sighed. His only consolation was that

things were getting back to normal at Ewing Oil and he would have the privilege of handling this Ames and Garr problem according to his own best counsel. That meant he could be far more "creative" than if he had someone looking over his shoulder all day long.

J.R. shuddered when he thought about the past year, when Bobby married Pamela Barnes. J.R. never could figure out how Bobby could have married the daughter of the man the Ewings hated so much—Digger Barnes. Encouraged by Pam, and with the blessings of their daddy, Bobby had actually tried his hand as co-president of Ewing Oil, a title he still held.

It had not been easy for J.R. to convince Bobby that the oil business just wasn't for him. He hadn't been able to convince him with words, actually, but with well-placed actions here and there. A false report here, a little sabotage there. And now, finally, it looked like Bobby was seeing the light.

Bobby was focusing more and more on construction projects, which was fine with J.R., because he felt those projects were certainly doomed to failure. In J.R.'s not so humble estimation, Bobby just wasn't a businessman, and it would have been easier on all concerned if he could have just recognized that about himself early on. Squeezing him out of Ewing Oil had really been the kindest thing he could have done for his baby brother, J.R. thought. And all he really had had to do was put a little burr under Bobby's saddle and tell the horse to git!

After all, J.R. reasoned, *I'm the first born*

and the one who brought Ewing Oil into the modern age. No one was going to take it away from him! Not even his blood brother!

But now, with Bobby pointed in another direction, the pressure on J.R. was leveling off. Bobby still came to the office and liked to feel he knew what was happening with Ewing Oil, but he was no longer a serious threat. Finally, J.R. was free to run the business the way he saw fit.

Pacific Avenue was particularly crowded, maybe because it was the balmy, breezy, sunny type of day that Dallas residents love. Many secretaries, executives, receptionists, and mail-room clerks had left their offices early so that they could enjoy a stroll along the avenue before they went to lunch. Pacific Avenue is like Fifth Avenue in New York, a thoroughfare that cuts through the heart of town, lined with the largest corporations and poshest shops in town.

Bobby Ewing was making his way through the crowd as quickly as he could. The Cattleman's Club tended to fill up early at lunch, and since Bobby wanted to spread out with some papers before he met his architect, he wanted to get there before the mob. He had important choices to make on his latest construction project, a group of seven homes in Tuckahoe, about forty miles north of Dallas, and he wanted to review the material the landscape engineer had given him before he made a final decision about the size of the outdoor terraces for each house.

About a block from the restaurant, he heard a man call out his name in a sudden, loud shout.

"Bobby Ewing! Heads up!" the voice commanded.

Turning around, Bobby saw a football sailing straight to him over the heads of the thronging passersby. Automatically, the Ewing son leaped high into the air, stretched out his arms and made the catch with a dense thud.

What in the world was happening? Bobby wondered, as he cradled the ball in his hands and searched the crowd to find the man who had thrown it. He had seen many things in downtown Dallas, but a football pass on Pacific Avenue had not been one of them.

Bobby continued looking through the crowd. There was no clue to who might have made the throw. Then he looked down at the ball and broke out in a wide grin. It was worn, and on its side he read words written long ago in indelible ink: "Texas 14—Colorado 7." Scattered around the score were the scrawled signatures of an entire football team, a team Bobby knew was made up of a very special bunch of guys. They had all been his teammates at the University of Texas years ago!

The ball could belong to only one person —Taylor "Guzzler" Bennett, captain of the team and Bobby's best college buddy. Bobby looked up now, expectant excitement on his face.

"Guzzler! Guzzler Bennett! Where the hell are you?" he yelled, standing against the flow of traffic. A few passersby bumped into him, but he just grinned and muttered apologies, his eyes still searching the changing crowd for the man who must have thrown the ball.

Suddenly the crowd parted, and a tall, massively built man appeared. He looked to be a couple of years older than Bobby, with a weathered face and fluffy salt-and-pepper hair. The man's arms spread wide open, and suddenly Bobby was folded inside a big bear hug.

"Bobby Ewing! Bobby!" the man said, his voice full of emotion.

Bobby broke away from the hug to take in his old friend. But he held on to the man's arms as he looked in his face.

"Guzzler Bennett! It had to be you! Only you would ever toss a pass in the middle of a crowded street!" he gushed.

"Yup," the man answered and smiled. "And only *you* would actually catch it!"

"This is incredible, Guzzler!" Bobby exclaimed. "I can hardly believe it's really *you!*"

Guzzler threw his head back and laughed happily.

"Well, Bobby—this handsome face, fantastic body, the dazzling smile, the silvery mane—who else could it be? I figure God threw my blueprints away when I turned out so pretty, so there's only one of me!"

Suddenly a small woman, who had been walking with her eyes down, bumped into Bobby. "Watch where you're going! You can't just stop in the middle of the street like this and have a little chat! What are you, crazy?" she said loudly, before she brushed herself off and went on.

"Well, I suppose she's right! If this is a college reunion we'd best not have it out in the street like this!" Bobby said, suddenly sensitive to the people being inconvenienced by two men blocking the walkway.

"Actually, I was on my way to your office, little buddy. Thought you might like this little present," Guzzler said, referring to the football. "You know, you won the game single-handedly that day, and I've always sort of felt you should have this. You're the one who really deserves it."

Bobby said nothing. He just smiled, packed the football under one arm and wrapped the other around his old friend's shoulder. "Come on, Guzz," he said warmly "I'm going to take you someplace where we can talk and do a little catching up on old times."

"Fine with me! I'm thirsty!" Guzzler said and laughed as Bobby led him by the arm to the Cattleman's Club.

After lunch the football lay on the table like a centerpiece amid the empty dishes. Guzzler sat alone, finishing a brandy. Just then the waitress arrived with another.

"Your timing is perfect. And I might say the same for your form, young lady," Guzzler said flirtingly, switching his glass with the one on the waitress's tray.

Bobby returned to the table and took his place by his half-full brandy.

It was a good thing I called. Architects are sensitive types. They think you hate them if you're late for a meeting."

"Architects, eh?" Guzzler mused. "You and your new bride thinking of building a house?"

"No, Guzzler," Bobby answered. "You see,

I've gotten myself involved in the construction business. I'm starting small, with only a couple projects until I learn the ropes, then I'm thinking of branching out and starting 'Ewing Construction.' I tried working at Ewing Oil, but I just found I needed something of my own."

"Oh? Is your daddy still the CEO at Ewing?" Guzzler asked, the alcohol appearing to have no effect on him. "He must be moving up in years, now, I would imagine."

"No, Daddy had a heart attack, so he spends most of his time ranching. He's fine now. In fact, I haven't seen him so vibrant and alive in years. But Mama wanted him out of the fray, so to speak, and he's really taken to ranching. It's J.R. who is running the business, by himself, mostly."

Guzzler snorted and laughed at the mention of J.R.'s name.

"Lordy, lordy, I forgot all about him! Mister Wonderful himself!" he joked ironically. "No wonder you want to get the hell out of Ewing Oil!"

Guzzler's remark was incredibly perceptive, Bobby thought. Nevertheless, he issued a mock warning to his old friend. "Now, now, Guzzler. He's still my big brother. Better watch what you say."

Guzzler just smiled sheepishly. "Fair enough, little buddy," he agreed, finishing his brandy in a large gulp.

"So, 'Ewing Construction,' huh?" he continued, more serious now. "Well, that sounds great, just great. I knew you'd win and win big no matter what you did, Bobby. You're a natural. You always were a winner through and through." Guzzler laughed and patted the football. "Never, ever in my entire life will I ever forget your eighty-yard run that day! If the Cowboys' recruiters were in the stadium that day, you'd probably be a football star today —and the construction business would have lost one of its shining stars."

Bobby might have noticed now that the alcohol was reaching Guzzler, but he had had more than his usual one drink himself and life seemed terribly sweet. "Well, I find it hard to believe you would hold on to that ball all these years for me." Bobby laughed.

"Why not?" Guzzler asked. "You were the best quarterback who ever played on my team."

"Well, let's not forget that I would have never even made the team if you hadn't coached me," Bobby added modestly.

Guzzler stood up, but quickly sat down again. "Now, don't go giving me an award for recognizing talent! Bobby, you were the kind of kid who has a ton of ability and an ounce of confidence. Once we built your confidence up, you were home free. That's really all you needed," Guzzler said sincerely.

"Well, that may be—or it may be you taught me the whole damned game. But it really doesn't matter, Guzzler. You were great to me in those days. And I don't think I would be doing so well today if I hadn't known you then. Just having someone that I could really talk to—I mean, we really had some special times, you and me."

Guzzler leaned intimately across the table as the other diners began to glance their way. His voice took on a dramatic stage whisper. "Bobby, please," he teased, "don't start crying. I can't stand to see a grown man cry."

Bobby smiled as the waitress appeared again, this time with the check, which she carried on a small black tray.

"Gentlemen, is there anything else I can do for you?" she asked.

"Oh, honey—" Guzzler joked, "you could do a lot for me, but I don't think your boss would approve of any of it!"

"We'll just have the check, please," Bobby said.

But as the waitress left the tray, Guzzler grabbed the check and said, "Wait a minute, Bobby. This one is on me."

"Not so fast," Bobby responded, snatching it out of his friend's fingers. "I owe you a lot more than this, Guzzler, and you know it."

Bobby reached down and signed the check as he asked, "So, Mr. Bennett, what brings you to our fair city and just how long will you be in Dallas?"

"Just a few days, Bobby," Guzzler answered as they got up from the table. Bobby picked up the ball and placed it under his arm. "I have a few meetings with bankers."

"Are you going to start some new drilling?" Bobby asked.

"Nope!" Guzzler laughed as they headed for the exit. "Would you believe I'm raising some cash for a project in Venezuela? I'm building a few hundred high-rises in Caracas. That place is *hot*, Bob! There's an incredible need for housing there, and an international community that can really afford the best."

"High-rises?" Bobby asked incredulously as he held the door open for his friend. "You're not telling me you're in construction, too?" he asked.

"Sure am. For the past couple years in fact." Guzzler smiled as they exited onto the busy thoroughfare.

"Well, tell me all about it," Bobby insisted enthusiastically as they walked back in the direction of the Ewing Building. "Why did you make the change?"

Guzzler smiled. "Gosh. Time sure does fly. We've been out of touch for what, six, seven years now? A lot of time, a lot of changes. I got married. You got married. I got divorced."

Bobby's eyes were as large as half-dollars. "You, Taylor-the-Guzzler-Bennett? You actually got married? Well, I would like to meet the woman who caught you! You married! I can hardly believe it. It's an unbelievable thought."

"Well, Bobby, you're one-hundred-percent right about that. It was truly unbelievable. And after a while, I couldn't believe it and neither could she! That's been over for about four years now," Guzzler admitted without pride. "And I won't ever make that mistake again."

Bobby didn't want to pry, so he changed the subject. Undoubtedly, his friend would fill him in on the details later.

"Guzzler, where are you staying?" Bobby asked, as if on a whim.

"Why, the Fairview, of course. Only the best for yours truly," he answered.

"Well, you're going to do better than best," Bobby told him. "Come on. You're checking out and coming to Southfork."

"No, Bobby," Guzzler protested. "I don't want to impose on you and your family—"

But before he could say more, Bobby grabbed him by the arm and walked with him to the street. "Taxi! Taxi!" Bobby called, raising his arms to attract a cab. "No arguments, you hear? You're coming to Southfork and that's that. When my best friend comes to Dallas, he doesn't have to stay in some hotel."

"Bobby, now I insist," Guzzler said. "The Fairview is just fine for me. I'll only be here a few days anyway and . . ."

Bobby wasn't having any of it. "I said 'no arguments.' Stop being so polite—it doesn't suit you."

"Well, okay, but I can't come right away. I have an appointment this afternoon. I'll take a cab out myself tonight."

"Okay," Bobby said. "But make sure you're there in time for dinner, you hear?"

"Aye! Aye! Yes, sir, little buddy. Dinner it is!"

The two men grabbed hands briefly and then parted company on the busy street.

Southfork, the Ewing family ranch, looked especially magnificent at dusk, when the setting sun cast its colorful rays over the rambling mansion. Pam Ewing, Bobby's bride of almost a

24

year, leaned against a pillar in the front of the house so she could watch the spectacle in all its glory while her husband tried to fill her in about his old friend.

"Wait till you meet him, Pam. He's great. He was like a big brother to me in school, taught me the ropes and really helped me out. I was really shaky those years. Growing up with J.R. as a big brother, well, it was hard—but when Guzzler came along . . ."

The sun was just taking its final bow, a slow glorious descent, shimmering pink, orange and lavender across the sky.

"Well, where is he?" Pam asked and smiled.

"He'll be here. He's just a little late, that's all. He has business in town. He's got himself involved in construction too, Pam. He's building high-rises in Caracas. Apparently there's a real housing crunch there and he wants to cash in—"

Just then the horn of a cab honked and drove up the long driveway to Southfork's main entrance. Guzzler jumped out, carrying a small suitcase, and bounded up the steps of the mansion as the driver called out, "Twenty-two fifty, mister."

"Fine," Guzzler responded, turning back. "I'll pay in traveler's checks if that's okay with you."

But just as Guzzler reached for his pocket, Bobby broke from Pam and hurried up to the driver, pressing three crisp tens into his hand. "Keep the change," the Ewing son murmured.

"Wait a minute! Lunch *and* a cab ride? That makes two I owe you, Bobby!" Guzzler said.

"Don't worry. You'll get a bill at the end of the month," Bobby responded as he picked up his friend's suitcase and started to the house.

"Guzzler, I'd like you to meet the most wonderful woman who has ever lived. My wife, Pam. Pam, this is Taylor Bennett, affectionately known as the Guzzler," he said, smiling happily.

Pam reached out her hand and smiled sweetly. "I'm happy to meet you. Bobby speaks so highly of you, Guzzler," she said sincerely.

"Likewise," Guzzler added. "And I must say, Bobby told me you were quite beautiful, and he was absolutely right."

"Thank you," Pam answered, flattered.

"But you shouldn't let your husband throw around his money on cab rides like that, Pam. I'd suggest you put that boy on a budget. Maybe four or five dollars a day for lunch and gas!" he added with a twinkle in his eyes.

All three of them were laughing happily at the joke as they walked through the big carved wooden doors of Southfork.

Chapter Two

The Ewing family sat around their large mahogany table as Raoul cleared the dinner plates and began pouring coffee and serving fresh strawberries with cream in fine crystal bowls. The eyes of all the Ewings were riveted on their guest, Guzzler Bennett.

"And, who was with me in the Rolls, but Christina," he said, enjoying the impending climax of the story he was telling. "And I knew that if her daddy caught us together, my shipping deal would really go down the drain! Then I see a photographer—a real paparazzi—and he's kinda sneaking up to the limo in one of those little Vespas that they have over there in Greece. So I jump right over the back seat and into the driver's seat—'cause the driver was off buying cigars or something—and I gunned the engine and took off straight ahead. But what I didn't know was that there was a sewer under construction right in front of us, and all of a sudden—whooo—me and Christina were up to our eyeteeth in you-know-what and she says to me, 'You Americans really know how to treat a girl, don't you?'"

With that everyone around the table, except J.R., burst into laughter.

Miss Ellie's pleasure was due only partially to Guzzler's amusing stories, which all seemed to feature only himself and the very rich and famous. Mainly, she was happy to see Bobby enjoying himself so. Guzzler Bennett had been a good friend to her son when he was in school, and it was a real pleasure for her to have him back at Southfork. Jock, too, had always been fond of the boy and seemed to enjoy seeing him again.

As for Lucy, the girl was absolutely mesmerized by Guzzler. Laughing with undisguised pleasure at his every little joke—funny or not —Lucy tossed her long blond hair over one shoulder and then the other in the hope of catching Guzzler's attention. After all, Lucy thought, she wasn't a little girl anymore. She was an eighteen-year-old woman!

Ellie watched Lucy act out the mannerisms of a child-woman. She wondered what Lucy's father, Gary, would think of her today. Gary was Ellie's middle son, who, because of a series of altercations with Jock and J.R., had left the family and moved to California.

J.R.'s wife, Sue Ellen, listened to the stories with polite but detached amusement. Newly pregnant and in love with another man, Sue Ellen lived more for the odd moments when she could phone her lover than for anything else. But her eight-year marriage to J.R. was still a strong source of security and even identity for her. Taking a cue from J.R., who was definitely not amused, she allowed herself only to smile demurely at Guzzler's tales.

Pam was drinking in every word. At last she'd had the chance to meet the famous Guzzler Bennett. At least he was famous with Bobby. When he and Pam were first dating, Bobby had mentioned Guzzler one night and expressed sorrow that he had fallen out of touch with his old friend. Pam had encouraged Bobby to try to find Guzzler, but his subsequent efforts had been futile. Now, seated next to Bobby, Pam basked in the warmth her husband was exuding for his old friend. *If only Guzzler weren't quite so loud,* she thought, although she liked his spirited ways.

Coffee over, and dessert eaten, the family got up from the table and started for the living room.

As they made their way to the other room, Jock threw his arm around his son's friend and invited him for a brandy. "Let's see if you're the drinking champion you used to be, Guzzler," he said with a chuckle.

"Well, well, well," Guzzler said, enjoying the attention he was getting from the Ewing family, "that sounds like a right good idea to me, Jock!"

With that, Lucy grabbed Guzzler's arm and looked up into his eyes. "Mind if I join you?" she cooed. Then she quickly turned to her grandfather and added, "Not for a brandy, Grandpa, just for the company."

Guzzler looked at her and laughed softly. "Do I mind? Well, I should say not, Lucy! You've really grown up since I saw you last! I feel like Maurice Chevalier—'Zank Heaven for leetle girls!'"

At the entrance to the living room, J.R. put his hand on his wife's arm. "Well, darlin'—I think I'll head upstairs, I've had about all the name-dropping I can stand in one evening," he said quietly.

"Well, if you don't mind, J.R., I think I'll stay down here for a while," Sue Ellen said demurely. "I find the man fascinating."

"Is that so? I find the man annoying," J.R. grumbled.

Sue Ellen and J.R. looked at one another coldly for the briefest second. They had a code between them. While together in public, they were impeccably polite to each other. But behind closed doors, they revealed their true bitterness and animosity. Sue Ellen had recently confessed that the child she was carrying might not be his. All of J.R.'s rage had been useless. What could he do? His father and mother were longing for a grandson. To divorce Sue Ellen when she was finally pregnant would be unconscionable. The child would be born and raised as a Ewing with no one the wiser—ever.

J.R. issued a polite but cold good-night to the rest of his family and grumpily strode upstairs to look over some financial papers.

"I'll be right up, darlin'," Sue Ellen called out for the benefit of her in-laws. But instead of following the rest of the family into the living room, she slipped into Jock's study and headed straight for the phone.

"Hello, Cliff," she said into the receiver. "Of course it's me, darlin'." She laughed quietly. "He's upstairs. Bobby has an old friend visiting and apparently he's somebody J.R. never liked. But then, J.R. doesn't like many people." Sue Ellen was laughing happily now. "No, darlin', I don't think he likes you very much either. But don't worry, because I like you very, very, very much, and I can't wait to see you. I can't tomorrow, how about Sunday? J.R. has some sort of meeting in the morning."

Just then Lucy came into the room to get a bottle of brandy that Jock kept stored away in his study closet for special occasions.

Lucy heard Sue Ellen talking on the phone to her hairdresser. *Odd to make an appointment for a Sunday,* Lucy thought, but then, Sue Ellen's appearance meant a lot to her. *Guess it's not easy being a former Miss Texas,* Lucy mused.

"Oh, no, Dorothy. The look is wonderful. I just need about a half inch cut off the back. Yes, Sunday is good for me. At ten then." And with that, J.R.'s wife hung up the phone, smiled sweetly at her niece and left the room.

Bobby's football was on the living-room coffee table as Pam, Bobby, Ellie, Jock and Guzzler sat sipping their brandies.

"The thing I still don't quite understand, Guzzler, is *why* you left the oil business. It sounds like you were doing so well," Bobby said, trying to figure out his friend.

"Oh, Bobby—don't misunderstand me. I'm

not out of oil, not by any means! It was just that my wells were doing *so* well, and the money was pouring in so strongly and steadily, that I figured it was time to branch out. I think it was C.P. Snow, the British scientist, who said, 'A life without change is an unexplored life.'"

Lucy gazed at Guzzler, her blue eyes large and warm. "I would imagine that you would be successful at whatever you do. You just know so much about everything!" she gushed.

Guzzler's eyes crinkled on the sides. "Lucy, I just wish that were true. It seems to me that everything I learn just shows me that there's a lot more to learn! But then, I guess that's what life is for—learning."

Everyone was silent as they contemplated Guzzler's statement.

After a moment, he looked up. "Gosh, folks," he said, charmingly self-conscious. "Maybe I should go upstairs. I've been yakking here all night and your poor ears must be tired!"

Ignoring him, Bobby suddenly picked up the football that Guzzler had given him earlier in the day. "Come on, Guzzler! Let's have a little night game! I want to see if you can still catch the ball!"

Guzzler smiled, ready to meet the challenge, and the two men headed for the door. On the way out, Jock slapped his son's friend on the back. "Guzzler, now that you're here, I hope you'll stay for a while!"

"Yes, Guzzler. Stay as long as you like! We love having you," Miss Ellie added, smiling.

"Agree! I think that would be terrific!" Lucy

added as flirtatiously as she could with her grandparents present.

Guzzler was sincerely touched by the Ewings' warmth and hospitality. Turning to Bobby he remarked lightly, "You know something, you have one hell of a family."

Bobby grinned and headed to the door, football in hand, as Pam looked on in amazement.

"Bobby? It's dark out! How can you play football?" she asked.

"That's nothing. I'll just have Raoul put the lights on. We used to do this all the time at school. Right, Guzzler?"

Guzzler looked at Pam sheepishly. "It's true, we did," he said with a shrug as the two men headed for the door.

"Well, fine," Pam said emptily. This wasn't quite the kind of evening she had envisioned when Bobby called to say Guzzler Bennett would be coming out for dinner, but if it made Bobby happy . . .

Jock stood at the bottom of the main stairway, his hand resting lightly on the carved wooden rail. "Ellie? Are you coming up?" he asked his wife.

"Teresa had to leave early tonight, Jock. I think I'll just go in the kitchen and make sure everything is put away."

"If you'd like the company, Miss Ellie, I can help you," Pam said, and her mother-in-law smiled. Pam may have been a Barnes, but she was a lovely person and a wonderful daughter-in-law.

"Thank you, Pam. That would be nice."

The two women walked through the dining room to the kitchen, where they began sorting out the china and cutlery. Pam could hear her husband and Guzzler on the back lawn, shouting and running happily.

"Miss Ellie, I'm surprised that J.R. isn't out there throwing the ball around. I thought he loved things like that! But he just seemed to disappear after dinner," Pam remarked casually.

Miss Ellie reached for a china tureen as her daughter-in-law put away dessert dishes. "Pam, I think J.R. is jealous of Guzzler Bennett," she replied, a far-off look in her eye. "You know, when Bobby and J.R. were growing up, J.R. seemed to have more than the usual amount of sibling rivalry. I think he never really adjusted to having a baby brother. Oh, he tried to be a good big brother. But somehow, he always botched it! Even when they were very little, J.R. would tell Bobby what to do—which balloon to choose at the fair, or which color socks to put on. And naturally, Bobby resented it.

"But, when Bobby went to college and met Guzzler, Guzzler became the older brother Bobby had always wanted. It was as if Bobby didn't have the time for two big brothers, and he preferred Guzzler. I guess J.R. got squeezed out there for a while. I know J.R. was hurt by that, though he would never show it. Not openly, anyway."

Pam was surprised by everything her mother-in-law was telling her. In the year since she had come to Southfork as Bobby's bride, it seemed to her that J.R. did everything in his power to be a terrible brother to Bobby. At work he had constantly frustrated his younger brother by ignoring all Bobby's ideas and keeping him in the dark about important deals.

Bobby's frustration and rage had grown to the point that he had finally thrown up his hands and come up with this construction idea. He desperately needed work of his own, and an identity of his own.

On a more personal level, J.R. consistently refused Pam and Bobby anytime they invited him or Sue Ellen to go anywhere. He would always apologize, offer a weak excuse, and that would be that.

"I'm surprised to hear this, Miss Ellie. It seemed to me that J.R. wouldn't care much one way or another what Bobby did or who he knew."

Miss Ellie's forehead wrinkled. "You know, Pam, deep down J.R. is a very sensitive person. But I think it's easy to misunderstand him because he doesn't let that sensitivity show very often."

"No, he certainly doesn't" was all Pam could say as she continued putting things away.

The next morning, Bobby woke Guzzler up early so that he could drive him out to the new construction site and show off his latest project.

As Bobby's red Mercedes approached the site, he found himself beaming with pride. Two months ago the land had been nothing but scrub. Now, there were the frames for seven fine houses, and the bulldozers had already started the landscaping process, leveling the soil for lawns and gardens.

Stopping the car near the construction site, Bobby and Guzzler got out and walked over to the empty frames.

"If it weren't Saturday, I'd introduce you to the roofer. He's a terrific guy. He did my Home for Wayward Boys a few months ago. By the way, these houses are already sold. They sold out on the blueprints alone. I had a waiting list as long as your arm!" Bobby looked at his old friend with pride.

"Well, what do you think?" Bobby asked eagerly as Guzzler squinted against the sun to examine the house sites.

"It's a good thing your roofer is using tile," Guzzler said. "I had a devil of a time with those composition shingles. They cheapen a place, and worse, they just don't last!" he said, his eyes surveying the properties like a hawk's.

"Yeah. But what do you think—about the whole project, I mean?" Bobby asked again.

Guzzler narrowed his eyes speculatively. "To tell you the honest truth, Bobby, I think you're on the wrong track," he said gently.

Bobby's face fell. This was the first negative comment he had heard about this latest venture, and it stung. That was the kind of comment he would expect from J.R., not from his best friend. "Thanks a lot," Bobby retorted. "That's just what I was hoping to hear from you. I mean, this is only my second project. I'm still learning. I think I have the right to some mistakes."

"Now, wait a minute, Bobby. You asked me a

question and I gave you the most honest answer I could."

"Well, it wasn't exactly the answer I wanted to hear," Bobby said truthfully, the hurt look still lingering in his eyes. "And frankly, I don't know where you're coming from. This project has proceeded along with almost no problems! It's been a success from day one! To me, anyway."

Guzzler chuckled and shook his head. "Bobby, Bobby," he murmured, "keep your shirt on. Now, you say that other project of yours—the home for boys—you say that project finished eight weeks early and came in twenty-two thousand under budget, right?"

Bobby nodded, confused and hurt.

"Then," Guzzler continued, "you got involved with this one. You had somebody draw up plans to your specifications and bango! You sold them all out, right?"

"Yeah . . ." Bobby commented.

"And in the car coming here, you were talking about doing another development with ten homes when this is done, right?"

"So," Bobby asked, "what are you leading up to?"

Guzzler laughed and shook his head. Then, flinging his arm around Bobby's shoulder, he said, "It's just like when you were in school, little buddy! No confidence! What the hell are you doing fooling around with a pint-sized project like this? You've got a track record, boy!"

Bobby looked astounded. "Guzzler, this is my second project! I'm just getting my feet wet! I have a lot to learn yet!" he insisted.

"Little buddy! You say you're just getting started, but I'm telling you, you outdistanced people who have been in the business for twenty years! Why are you fooling around with piddly stuff like this? You're ready for the big time, boy! Look at it this way—you're putting in all the time and energy. So why not put it in on something big? Make a name for yourself! Lap up a little glory! Instead of going on to a ten-house tract next project, go for the gold! Build four, five hundred houses. Or a skyscraper downtown. Two of 'em!"

Bobby laughed now, relieved by his friend's excessive enthusiasm.

"Well, sure I'd like to work up to something like that, but right now, I would need help. I'm too green. Maybe if I had someone with experience . . ."

Guzzler was walking ahead toward the building sites. As Bobby watched him from the back, it hit him like a thunderbolt!

"Guzzler! You! I mean, you and me! We would make the perfect team for a big project! Perfect!" he shouted enthusiastically.

Guzzler turned around and frowned.

"Bobby. Come on. You don't need me or anybody. Besides, I'm tied up. I've got that Caracas deal and other projects all over the world."

"So what?" Bobby asked.

"So what?" Guzzler echoed in disbelief. "Look, I can't horn in on a Ewing project!"

But Bobby was undaunted. "Come on, Guzz. Leave that to the attorneys. Tell you what, we could form a subsidiary! Ewing and Bennett! It's perfect!"

"Bobby, Bobby," Guzzler said, shaking his head. "They need me in Caracas!"

"Great! You and I will spend a little time scouting projects here, and when we come up with one we both like, you go to Caracas and I'll start the field operations! They have telephones in Venezuela, don't they?"

"Well, I suppose I could postpone South America for a few weeks, anyway," Guzzler said seriously. "But are you sure you want to work with an old dog like me?"

"Am I sure?" Bobby asked happily. "I'm more than sure! Today Dallas, tomorrow—Fort Worth! Come on! It's time to celebrate!" he shouted, as the two men scampered toward the car, laughing all the way.

The idea of forming a partnership was so sudden and so appealing, that neither Bobby nor Guzzler noticed the blue late-model Chevy that had turned onto the scrubland across the highway and parked with the motor running.

"How the hell am I supposed to focus the camera this far away?" a young man asked angrily.

"That's why we got the telephoto lens, stupid!" a woman replied. "And since your hands are shaking so bad, let me snap the picture! You're just too damned incompetent!"

"Take it easy, you two!" a second, older man said. "This one ain't even the one we really want. It's his brother! And we'll have other times to get his picture when we get to the oil building."

"Oh, he's coming straight into view. Which one is this again?" the woman asked.

"Dark hair, tall. Bobby James Ewing. He's the youngest one," the man answered.

"My, my, he sure is pretty!" the woman commented as she snapped a series of photos.

Pam Ewing lay in bed, a look of deep concern on her face. The luminous numbers on her clock seemed to shout "3 A.M." when she glanced at it. Where was Bobby? It wasn't like him to stay out so late. When he'd called about midnight, he had said he'd be home soon.

Pam rolled over, picked up her pillow and reshaped it before she rolled over again and tried to sleep. It was no use—"3:07."

Just then a car pulled up the long driveway to Southfork and screeched to a halt, disturbing the peace of the night.

Pam sat up in bed, then rose and pulled on her white terry robe. This had to be him, she thought as she hurried downstairs.

The car that had pulled up was a yellow taxicab. As Pam watched from the veranda, one door opened and Guzzler Bennett came spilling out. Then, moving unsteadily on his feet, he walked around the car to help Bobby.

"All right, little buddy, here's my hand. Just grab it and hold on," he mumbled.

Pam watched in amazement as Bobby's hand reached for his friend's and grabbed on to it, like a person's caught in quicksand.

"Thanks, Guzzler," Bobby said, his inebriation obvious. "I think my toes got paralyzed or something. I can't feel my socks either."

Then, with a pull, Bobby was up on his feet, but not for long. Once out of the cab, he slid to the ground, and Guzzler had to pick him up again.

"You know something, Guzzler?" Bobby asked, his voice filled with the slobbering sentimentality of too much alcohol. "You're a pal. And you know something else, Guzzler? You were right about the drinking. I *can't* keep up with you."

As he moved to the door, Pam noticed that Bobby could hardly walk. He was a pathetic sight. Pam opened the door to assist the two men. She was noticeably upset as she stood there, her face illuminated only by the light of the full moon.

"Uh-oh!" Guzzler called out in a loud whisper. "Bobby, there's a woman waiting up for you!" he said with a slur.

Bobby looked alarmed for a second, then giggled.

"Don't let her know I'm drunk, okay, Guzz?" he said. And with that, Bobby collapsed inside the doorway.

"Bobby! Are you okay?" Pam cried as she rushed to him.

But Bobby was beyond response. He had passed out cold.

Like a knight from an old fairy tale, Guzzler Bennett took the opportunity to bow before Pam. "My lady—we seem to have disgraced ourselves mightily. Would you but forgive us and we will never err again!"

Pam looked at her husband's friend but said nothing.

"And, in order to make amends for this deed most dastardly, I shall be more that happy to dispose of your husband's remains," Guzzler continued irrationally.

"Take him to the bedroom please, Guzzler," Pam asked in a firm tone.

"But of course, madame, of course," he said, hoisting the unconscious Ewing to his shoulder and trudging up the steps with him as a worried Pam hurried along behind.

In the bedroom, Guzzler managed to get Bobby to the bed and drop him on it safely. Then, proud as a boy scout, he turned to Pam and grinned.

"Thank you, Guzzler. Good night," Pam said.

But Guzzler didn't leave the room. He seemed riveted to the spot for a moment as he stood in front of her.

"You are beautiful," he said, suddenly awed.

"Thank you and good night, Guzzler," Pam repeated, her patience lessening.

Guzzler stepped toward her and sloppily threw his arms around her.

"You smell like flowers," he murmured noisily in her ear. "Beautiful flowers. Kiss me."

Pam struggled to break free of the drunken man but without luck. Even inebriated, he was powerfully strong.

"Guzzler! Stop it! Bobby is my husband!" she protested.

"So what? I was married once too. Just because you're married, it doesn't mean you can't have a little fun now and then," he said, nuzzling her neck with his wet lips.

"Well, this is *not* fun! And I want you to get out of my bedroom!" Pam shouted, as she tried to push him away.

"Come on. I know you girls like to play hard-to-get. That's okay with me," he said before he pushed his face onto hers.

Pam bit his lip as hard as she could.

"Ow!" Guzzler screamed in pain. "Why the hell did you do *that!*"

"I'm sorry," Pam muttered uneasily, "but you are very drunk now, and you have to leave!"

Holding his lip with his hands, Guzzler backed out of the room.

"If you change your mind, you know where I am," he murmured clumsily.

"I won't change my mind," Pam answered coldly. "Good night."

"Well, it's your loss, lady," he whispered before he disappeared from the room. "Just too bad for you."

Chapter Three

On Sunday morning, J.R. and Sue Ellen stood on the stairs looking like the perfect American couple. They were two handsome people dressed to perfection in the style of the moment. Their genteel manners were as impeccable as their dress.

"What a shame, darlin', that you have to go to a business meeting on a Sunday," Sue Ellen was saying as she straightened her husband's tie.

"Well, don't you worry now, Sue Ellen, I'll be back before three." He *had* to be back before three because Ames and Garr and their people had to be off the land by the time Jock and Ellie got back from church.

"Let's see," he said, checking himself out. "I have my briefcase, I have all the papers . . . I guess I'm all set. You have an enjoyable brunch, Sue Ellen. Give my regards to Reverend Thornwood and Grace," J.R. said, offering his cheek to her.

"Thank you, dear, I will." Sue Ellen pecked his cheek perfunctorily and waited for him to get down the stairs and out the door.

It was ten-thirty. She had till two. That would give her approximately two hours of happiness with Cliff—the only two hours of happiness she would have all week. And, she thought, watching her husband descend the stairs, she intended to enjoy every wonderful minute.

Pam got up early and decided to let Bobby sleep it off while she worked out and had a swim. The early morning was the best time for a workout. After a night like the previous one, Pam especially wanted to work away some tension so that she could think about things more clearly.

After her vigorous exercise session in the cabana, she pulled out the floating chair and relaxed in the middle of the pool. Relaxing under the early Texas sun, looking up at the billowing clouds surrounding Southfork, she considered the best course of action.

Last night's events had worried her. What would she say to Bobby when she saw him this morning? What was the best way for a wife to handle such a thing? Pam wondered.

One thing was sure, she had to keep a lid on her emotions. The fact that she was furious about Bobby's coming home drunk was really less important than it seemed. After all, they had been married almost a year and nothing like that had ever happened before. It wasn't as if it were a pattern. Didn't everybody have the right to let off steam with an old friend now and then, as long as it wasn't an everyday occurrence? To express too much anger about it would just make her seem like a heavy-handed fishwife!

On the other hand, it was important, she thought, for Bobby to know how she felt. Marriage was for sharing, and they both had a right to know how the other felt—even if those feelings might be disturbing.

Then there was the matter of Guzzler and his lewd pass. Bobby seemed to think Guzzler Bennett was such a great guy! Did he know his "friend" was perfectly willing to betray him? He couldn't know, she thought. And was *she* the one who had to tell him?

Just thinking about the incident made Pam sick with anger. How dare this man come to their house, get Bobby drunk, get drunk himself and try to make love to her! Her cheeks reddened with rage.

Pam breathed out deeply for a moment and let herself go limp, safely supported by the floating chair.

Then there was another question: Was it fair to hold Guzzler's behavior "under the influence" against him? Her own father, Digger Barnes, was a good man, but an alcoholic. While under the influence, he had said and done things that hurt himself and the people around him time and again. When he sobered up he would beg for forgiveness—assuming he remembered the incident at all. Time and again she had extended her understanding to him. Couldn't she do it for Bobby's friend? After all, she didn't really know the man that well—maybe the pass was completely out of character for him, a rare occurrence, a one-time aberration. Because, worst of all, if she did tell Bobby, wouldn't that be destroying something he deeply treasured?

Her decision made, Pam sighed, relieved. She needn't say a word. She would forgive, and more, forget about Guzzler's pass. On the other hand, it was her responsibility to let Bobby know she didn't like his drinking to excess—not even occasionally.

Pam was so deep in thought that she didn't notice Guzzler walking across the patio in his bathing trunks and sliding into the far end of the pool. She lay filled now with a peaceful feeling, her mind resting easy as she enjoyed the show the clouds were putting on for her benefit, dancing across the Texas sky.

Suddenly she felt a hand gripping her leg!

"Oh, my God!" she screamed as she jumped up out of her chair, her heart beating with fear.

"Hi!" Guzzler said, popping up out of the water and acting like a salesman greeting a potential customer. "Nice morning, isn't it?"

Pam did not respond. Instead she swam to the edge of the pool and lifted herself out of the water without comment.

"Hey!" he called, sounding genuinely apologetic. "I didn't mean to scare you! If I did, I'm sorry."

How could Bobby possibly like such an oily character? Pam thought unkindly. Guzzler Bennett was about as grown up as an eight-year-old boy!

"Oh, yes, I'm sure you're sorry," she said, her voice full of sarcasm.

Turning to him so that the anger in her eyes would be fully visible, Pam was surprised to see a look of confusion on Guzzler's face.

"Is something the matter, Pam?" he asked, climbing out of the pool and walking toward her. "Honestly, I didn't mean to scare you. I guess that was a dumb thing to do."

Guzzler was now standing near her, but he stopped a few feet away as if to give her space.

Why was he feigning innocence? This morning's Guzzler was certainly a different person from the monster who had tried to kiss her the night before—but this person couldn't be trusted any more now than last night.

"Guzzler, I don't think I should have to tell you what's wrong after last night!" she said icily, determined not to have words with her husband's friend.

Guzzler looked confused for a moment, but then a wide grin spread across his face.

"Oh! I get it!" he said, almost relieved. "You mean taking Bobby out like that and letting him get plastered. To tell you the truth, Pam, Bobby and I got so caught up in having fun that I kinda forgot he was a married man! But we didn't get into any trouble, I swear. We just had a few drinks and went for a pizza. I guess we were pretty out of it by then. I burned my lip and didn't even know it. And then, we wound up in a club and had a few more drinks and you know how one drink can lead to another. . . ."

Had he really forgotten that he practically

attacked her last night? Pam wondered angrily. As he went on telling her more about the "boys' night out," she believed he really had.

Just then Pam and Guzzler heard a heavy splash at the other end of the pool. Bobby had come out of the cabana and jumped into the pool.

"Good boy, Bobby!" Guzzler shouted, "that's the best thing for you after a night like last night! Keeps the blood going!" And with that, Guzzler dove back into the pool and swam toward his old friend.

Bobby came up for air and moaned, "Oh, my head! How long have you been up this morning, Guzzler?"

"Oh, since about six this morning. Isn't that right, Pam?" he quipped with a wink to Bobby's wife.

"Six!" Bobby cried incredulously. "This guy is really something else, isn't he Pam?"

"Oh, yeah. Really something else," Pam answered dryly.

But neither Guzzler nor Bobby seemed to be aware of her annoyance or even to notice very much that she was there. They were off in a world of their own now, horsing around in the pool like two college kids.

"Come on, I'll race you!" Guzzler shouted.

"Pam! Join us!" Bobby called to his wife.

"No, no. That's okay," Pam said, tying her wraparound skirt and heading toward the house. "You boys play in the pool. I'll go upstairs and see if I can find a dolly!"

As she left, Bobby looked after her with a

puzzled look. But before he could think about his wife's feelings too much, Guzzler stole his attention.

"Okay! Last one to do six laps is a rotten egg!" he shouted, and Bobby automatically dove into the water for the race.

As the '77 Chevy moved along the highway facing Southfork, the man in the back seat dropped to the floor.

"That's him!" he cried. "The one with the beige jacket! Get him good, 'cause that's our boy!"

"Say, Al, how'd you know he was going to be here this morning, anyway?" the younger man asked.

"'Cause I'm a genius, all right? That's how" was the gruff reply.

"Well, slow down, Fay, I can hardly take a picture if you're moving so fast!" the young man's voice cried out to the driver.

"I can't do anything conspicuous, or they'll see me, Will. You know that! Besides, I'm only doing thirty," the woman replied.

"It feels faster than that to me!"

"Dumbbell!" came the older voice from the floor of the back seat. "That's fast film! You got a thousandth of a second! Just snap, and get as many as you can! I want to know what that cracker looks like from the left, right, front and back! And get him with his hat off for God's sake! Those ones of Bobby Ewing are all hat brim! Make it good! This one's going to be paying our rent for a long time to come, right, Fay?"

The woman smiled. "I don't know about you, but after this time, I'm not paying rent again as long as I live! He can cover all my hotel bills, 'cause I'm going to be living in better digs than rented flats! You and me are going to go first class all the way. Sail the seven seas, and stop in all the ports! Right, baby?"

"Now you're talking, sweetheart," the man chortled.

"Yeah. Yeah. You two mean if these pictures come out, anyways!" the younger man growled nervously from behind the camera.

Following behind Ames and Garr's brand-new white truck as they drove to Section Forty of Southfork, J.R. was worried. What if his daddy found out that there was a crew of fifteen men testing his old capped-up well? J.R. sighed. He didn't like being dependent on luck, but this time he had to hope that he wouldn't get caught.

Dust was rising from the place where the men were working a quarter mile away. When he got there, he wasn't going to waste a minute, J.R. vowed. They could get the information they wanted and then get the hell out!

Willie Joe Garr brought the truck to a halt and the men got out.

"Yo! There! Kylie!" Jeb called out to a heavy-set man in a yellow hard hat who carried a clipboard and pencil in hand.

"Mr. Garr!" the man replied. "Good morning!"

"This is Mr. Ewing, Frank. J.R.—Frank Kylie. I thought you might appreciate having a man from out-of-state look at our well. He's the best. Worked for Weststar last year in Brazil, right Kylie?"

"Yes sir," the man replied.

"Well, Mr. Kylie, what did you find?" J.R. asked in an attempt to hurry things along.

Kylie adjusted his hat and looked at the oil executive. "To tell you the truth, the well is in great shape. Getting a field operation going shouldn't be much trouble at all. Whoever capped the well seemed to know what they were doing. That's why we were able to run all the tests today."

"Yes," J.R. spoke hurriedly, "but what about the oil reserves under the land?"

Kylie touched his hat again. "Well, sir," he began roughly, "I can only give you a rough estimate, you understand, but everything we found today checked out with the old records. I'd estimate you could fill a hundred-gallon tank in about twenty minutes—maybe less. That works out to seven thousand barrels a day, conservatively speaking."

Kylie paused and looked at the retinue of businessmen around him.

"Gentlemen, in my professional opinion, this well is a dynamo," he said with a happy twinkle in his eye. "This is what people are always hoping I'm going to find."

J.R.'s face reflected his supreme pleasure.

Now the Panhandle deal could proceed without glitches.

As for Ames and Garr, they were like two little boys in front of the candy counter, their eyes as big as silver dollars!

Looking at them from the corner of his eye, J.R. couldn't help smiling. But when he spoke, his voice was cool and calm, the voice of the rational, detached businessman in search of the best monetary deal.

"Jeb? Willie Joe? Is that satisfactory to you boys?" he asked his awed partners.

Jeb Ames and Willie Joe Garr looked at J.R. as if he was a crazy man.

"Are you kidding?" Jeb shouted. "Seven thousand barrels a day? With that sitting in reserve, J.R., we can go with you all the way on the Panhandle deal! With pleasure!"

"I'll say!" his awed partner added. "You don't worry about us, J.R. We're just happy you came to us first, that's all!"

"Well, then, Mr. Kylie," J.R. said, flaunting his superiority more than just a little, "I'd appreciate it if you would put this place back together as if no one was ever here today! That's very important to me. And as for us, gentlemen, I do believe we're finished for the day."

And with that, J.R. strode to his silver-gray Mercedes and drove back to the ranch, smiling broadly.

In Bobby and Pam's bedroom, Pam had put up her hair and changed to casual Sunday clothes. It was still early, and she wasn't sure how she was going to spend the day. But if it was like all the other days since Guzzler Bennett had arrived, she thought with a touch of bitterness, she would be spending it alone. Thank goodness Guzzler Bennett would be gone in a few days!

Since Guzzler had arrived at Southfork, Pam had seen a whole new side to Bobby, and it was a side she didn't particularly care for. Guzzler seemed to bring out an immaturity in Bobby that Pam hadn't known existed.

Since she had met Bobby, he had always been a gentleman through and through. He had had depth and wisdom, and sensitivity toward others that was unparalleled in any other man she had known.

But with Guzzler, Bobby was reverting to some sort of macho behavior. And it didn't suit him, Pam thought, not in the least.

"Pam!" Bobby called as he came in the room and got ready to shower and change. "Can you believe it? He beat me by a good half a lap!"

"Oh?" Pam answered politely. The way she was feeling right now, she thought, it didn't matter one bit who won that stupid little contest.

Bobby was rummaging in his drawers and closet, selecting clothes for later in the day.

"Hey," he asked all of a sudden, "what was that little comment about finding a dolly?"

"Well," Pam answered dryly, "if we're all going to act five years old, I thought I would find myself a little something to play with! Why should I miss all the fun?"

Suddenly all of Pam's distant behavior this morning made sense to Bobby. Of course she

54

would be upset. Wouldn't *he* have been upset if the tables were turned?

"Pam, about last night, honey. I don't know what happened. We just got a little carried away. But it won't happen again. I promise you."

Pam looked at her husband with happy relief. Her Bobby was back!

"Thank you, honey," she said, her voice softening. With a sigh, she smiled at him warmly. "Bobby. Just tell me how long he's going to be here. If I know that I can handle everything."

Bobby put his hands on her shoulders. "Pam, I've asked him to stay on as long as he can. I had Connie cancel all my appointments for next week, and Guzzler and I are going to start scouting for a construction project. Something a little bigger than what I've been doing so far." Bobby's voice was so warm and enthusiastic that Pam couldn't understand at first what he was really talking about.

"I don't get it, honey. What do you mean, scout a construction project? I thought Guzzler was here for only a few days!" she said, trying to hide her growing concern.

"Well, that was the original plan, Pam, but yesterday I got to thinking that Guzzler and I would be the perfect partners for a really big construction company. I would have told you yesterday if I'd had the time. See, he has a lot of experience and I can use—"

Pam's head was reeling. "Partnership? You and Guzzler?" she repeated.

"Sure. We'll form a subsidiary to Ewing Construction and we can work together on everything," Bobby explained, surprised and confused that his wife's reaction was so negative.

"But, Bobby," Pam said, her eyes searching his face, "when you got the idea of the construction company it was because you wanted to be independent! You said you needed something all your own!" she protested.

"Yes, I did!" Bobby said firmly. "But that was then. Now that I have the chance to team up with an experienced partner like Guzzler, I'd be crazy to pass that by!"

"But it isn't what you wanted. You fought your daddy to get Ewing Construction and now you're tossing it away like a—a football!" she said, her voice beginning to quiver with emotion.

Bobby looked deep into his wife's eyes. "Pam! Pam!" he said. "Don't worry! I know what I'm doing. And it's a brilliant idea. I have the perfect partner. How many people can say that? We're really going to make something together."

Pam drew away from her husband's touch. "Oh, sure," she said bitterly. "Meet with the architects by day and go get plastered at night!"

"You know something, Pam," Bobby said after a moment, "you and J.R. have something in common. You're both jealous of my friendship with Guzzler. And I don't like that on you any more than I do on J.R.! Jealousy doesn't suit you, Pam. I think you should give it up."

"I am not jealous!" Pam shouted. "I'm not! Really! In fact, for a long time I've been hoping you would find a man for a friend. I think you need that. I just think you should choose your friends a little more wisely! Since Guzzler appeared on the scene you've been acting strange. And I don't like this new Bobby Ewing. Not one bit!" Pam couldn't hold her feelings back anymore.

"You're so jealous you can't even think straight! Why don't you just admit it? You'll feel a lot better!" Bobby shouted in return.

But Pam was too furious and frustrated to continue the conversation. "Just leave! I can't talk to you, so you might as well leave!" she said, her voice quavering with rage.

Bobby matched her rage. "Fine. I'll be happy to leave!" he shouted before he marched out of the room, slamming the door behind him.

Bobby was driving faster than usual down the black highway, and Guzzler was concerned.

"Hey, little buddy! Lighten up! All married people fight. And you can't blame the little lady. You know how women are—none of them like it when the boys stay out late. That's why I ditched the last Mrs. Bennett, in fact!"

Bobby slowed the car to a reasonable speed and felt the tension leaving his body.

"Yeah. I guess that's what was really bothering her," he murmured.

"So, bring home some flowers and she'll forget all about it. Now," he asked, "where are we exactly?"

Pointing to the flat scrubland to the right, and

the newly constructed tracts of houses to the left, Bobby explained, "We're still outside Braddock, actually."

"Wow!" Guzzler murmured. "Last time I was out here, this was all prairies! What's all this new construction?"

"Well," Bobby began, "what's happening is Dallas and Fort Worth are growing into a kind of metroplex like St. Paul and Minneapolis, or El Paso and Juarez. Pretty soon Braddock is going to be eaten up, I'm afraid."

Suddenly Guzzler removed the white cowboy hat from his head and glanced over at Bobby with the look of a man who'd just had a vision.

"Jumpin' jehosiphat! Pull over, little buddy! Stop the car!" he shouted jubilantly.

Bobby didn't hesitate to do as his friend ordered, but he seemed puzzled. "What's wrong, Guzz? What is it?" he asked.

Suddenly, Guzzler was out of the car and had vaulted over the fence alongside the road.

"This is it, little buddy! This is *it!*" he bellowed at the top of his lungs as he threw his hat high into the air.

"What?" Bobby asked. "What are you talking about?"

Guzzler tried to calm down, but it was hard. Finally he pulled himself together enough to take his friend by the arm and lead him out onto the prairie. "This is our project! This is our perfect project! Just look around you. We could search the world over and we'd never find a better place than right here," he said, his eyes shining with the vision.

"Perfect for what?" Bobby asked, looking hopefully for the source of his friend's enthusiasm but seeing nothing but scrub.

"Why, for a shopping center, of course! Look at those houses out there across the road! Well, those people are going to need things—tables, lamps, chairs, clothes, food, a tailor, a drugstore. Bobby! This is a 'can't fail' deal! We've got to find the owners and buy up this land!"

Bobby's face took on a sheepish look. "Well, I do know the owners. I know them quite well, in fact."

"Great!" Guzzler shouted. "Let's get back to Southfork and get on the horn. I want to sew this one up as fast as possible. An opportunity like this doesn't come along that often, boy!"

"Listen," Bobby said awkwardly. "We don't exactly have to go back to call the owners, because, well, I'm them. I mean, I will be. Guzzler, the land you're standing on is Southfork!"

"This? This is Southfork?" Guzzler said, laughing. "Well, I'll be! This project is more perfect than perfect! What is that well over there? Dry?"

Bobby squinted to see the capped well his grandfather had ordered closed before he was born. It stood right in the middle of the area where the shopping center would be built. "Oh, that. It wasn't dry. But Mama and Daddy don't want it drilled, ever. They've put it in their will in perpetuity."

"Well, well, wasn't that smart of them!" Guzzler said. "Because this land is for people! Or, it will be when we get done with it. Right, Bobby?"

Bobby's eyes searched the prairie. He didn't need a demographics chart to tell him that Guzzler's idea was a sure winner.

"Right, Guzzler!" Bobby agreed with a laugh, as the two men walked back to Bobby's car.

Chapter Four

During the ride back to the house, Guzzler and Bobby were quiet, each thinking of the shopping center and its possibilities. Getting Jock and Ellie's permission to build on the back section of Southfork land wouldn't be easy, Bobby thought. When the idea of going into construction had first occurred to Bobby, Jock had been strongly opposed to his youngest son's decision, and now, Bobby was going to be asking for a piece of family land to build on.

Bobby remembered the day he first took his father aside and told him about his new plan for himself. Jock had had a hurt look in his eyes as he'd struck out against his son. "Hell, Bobby! You are an oil man!" he had said. "You come from an oil family! Why do you want to go messing around in construction?"

But as the months had gone by and Bobby had continued to pursue his new interest, Jock had gradually, though reluctantly, come to respect his youngest son's decision. There was no doubt about it—the elder Ewing had thought as he'd observed his son—Bobby was a happier man than when he had been working with J.R. exclusively. And his son's happiness was of great importance to Jock. For no matter how hard he tried to deny it, Bobby was Jock's favored son and had been so since the day he was born. There was a special caring, a tenderness in his feelings for Bobby.

Bobby knew how much his daddy loved him and knew that his mother did, too. Miss Ellie cared about her son's happiness even before her own. But he would never want to take advantage of his parents' love for him, he thought, as he gripped the wheel of his red Mercedes and saw the big white house come into view. Jock and Ellie would have to be convinced that the shopping center was in *their* best interests as a family, and that it made sense strictly on a business level. Otherwise the deal was off.

"Guzzler," Bobby said, as he braked and turned off the ignition. "I'd like to talk to my daddy alone about this if you don't mind."

Guzzler looked startled for the moment. "Listen, Bobby. If you don't think this is a good deal, we can just call it quits right here. I don't want you to go into anything not feeling right about it."

"No, no," Bobby said, concerned that his partner had misunderstood him. "There's no doubt in my mind that a shopping center on that particular parcel is going to be a terrific money-maker."

"And I'm not just talking through my hat, Bobby," Guzzler responded quickly. "I built one in Florida that sent me reeling! People were throwing so much money my way that I had to duck!"

"Well, I just think I should talk to Daddy alone first. You understand," Bobby said before he lifted his lanky, muscular body from the car and walked toward the house.

Just then Lucy appeared on the porch, obviously having overheard the last part of the men's conversation.

"You mean, Guzzler is going to be alone today? How nice for me," she said boldly. "I'll make sure he has some company!"

Bobby took a deep breath, opened the door to the house, then turned to give Guzzler a victory sign before he walked in.

Jock was in his study, holding a small but expensive and beautifully crafted Remington sculpture of a rider on a bronco. Moving about the wood-paneled room, he tested it on one shelf and then another, as Bobby stood by his father's desk.

"Daddy," he began, "you know how quickly the area between Dallas and Fort Worth is growing. Soon, it's going to be one major suburb serving both cities. You said so yourself not long ago."

Jock was distracted. Placing the sculpture on his desk, he just nodded affirmatively and studied the piece.

"Yes, I believe I did say that, Bobby," he murmured, his attention still apparently on the sculpture. "No . . . not here. I'd keep banging into it every time I answered the phone."

"Well, Guzzler and I were thinking that a shopping center in that area would provide a definite service for the people who are going to be living there." Bobby took a breath before he went on. "And Daddy, there's a piece of Southfork land, Section Forty, that Guzzler and I think would be the ideal place for such a shopping center. It's right across from the highway and very central to the area."

"Southfork land? You want to build a bunch of stores on Southfork land?" Jock asked, putting the sculpture down for the moment.

"Well, sir, it's a piece of land that is completely undeveloped. It's not even used for grazing. I think this parcel could conservatively net us over ten million dollars within the space of a year," Bobby answered as calmly as he could.

"Ten million? That's a nice piece of money. But I don't know, Bobby. I don't want to be negative about this, but you know your mama. She loves the land—the more natural the better. And I can't help feeling this shopping center idea just isn't for her."

That was exactly the response Bobby expected from his father and it didn't ruffle him in the least.

"Well, I would agree with her, Daddy, except the land I'm talking about is so far from the house. I don't think it would really bother her at all once it's developed. Section Forty is a good three miles away."

Jock was still holding the sculpture, and now he turned his attention to it again, looking for the perfect spot for it. Finally, he put it on the end of a crowded bookshelf where there was just enough room to fit it.

"Here?" he asked his son helplessly.

"How about the shelf above it? You might be able to see it better," Bobby suggested. The higher shelf had only a few books and plenty of room for the piece.

Taking the bronze and moving it, Jock reflected. "You know, I used to think your mama was crazy not to want to develop Southfork. There's an incredible amount of oil under that section. But your mama stood firm. She didn't want the land torn up, not even for a fortune. And since I've gotten involved in ranching, I've got to admit I can understand how she feels. I'm not so eager to go slicing up the ranch either!"

Bobby smiled. Since his heart attack and bypass, Jock Ewing was a changed man. Working on the ranch with his foreman, Ray Krebbs, he had come to enjoy the land as he never had before. Bobby liked the change in his father. Jock was gentler, mellower and wiser because of it.

But Bobby was a young man, full of the ambition and fire of youth. He was married now. This was the time of his life for him to build his fortune and make a name for himself. And he had chosen construction as the best way to do it.

"Daddy, I'm not talking about slicing up Southfork. I'm talking about taking an unused portion and developing it and adding to the family's coffers. If I thought it was slicing, I wouldn't even be here talking to you. But Section Forty fronts the highway. You would never run cattle there. The land is just sitting idle and costing you property taxes," Bobby explained.

Jock stepped back and admired the new placement of the sculpture. It was good. Bobby had taste and good sense, even in something as small as that. Jock walked to his desk and sat behind it, his hand thoughtfully rubbing his chin for the moment.

"Bobby," he began, "when you first came to me with this whole construction idea of yours, I thought it was so much garbage. You asked me what I thought and I told you outright that we're an oil family, not a bunch of carpenters! But you went ahead and started getting involved anyway. Well, son—I like that! I like your fighting spirit. And you won. And, to tell you the truth, personally I'd be inclined to trust your judgment on this one now. But your mama's involved here. That's her land as much as mine. So, here's what I'd like to do. I want you to show me that parcel and tell me exactly what you want to do there, and then we'll go talk to your mama."

Bobby sighed with a smile. His father's suggestion was fair enough, more positive than he had anticipated. "That's fine with me, Daddy. We'll go look. In fact, what are you doing right now?" he asked his father.

"Why, you're not going to miss a beat, are you, Bobby?" Jock said, chuckling to himself with pleasure. "You want to rip Texas down on

Sunday and build her back up by Monday afternoon!" he said and laughed.

"That's 'cause I want to move on to Oklahoma Tuesday!"

"Well, hell!" Jock challenged, moving to get his jacket. "I'm ready! But I want to get J.R., too."

Bobby's face screwed up. "J.R.? Daddy, this is my project!"

"Yes, Bobby, it is," his father answered firmly. "But J.R. is involved. He's a Ewing, too. That'll be his land someday."

What his father was saying made perfect sense to Bobby, and so reluctantly he agreed. "Okay, Daddy. Whatever you want," he said, holding the door open for the older man.

Lucy was sitting on the edge of a white outdoor table, her eyes aglow as she listened to Guzzler Bennett. Guzzler sat in a chair by the table leaning close to her.

"So," she was saying as sultrily as she could, "are you saying you think foreign girls are better than American girls?"

Guzzler chuckled. "That's a tough question, Lucy. There's some mighty fine women on both sides of the Atlantic. But there definitely is a special charm to a foreigner—"

"Well, tell me this, then," Lucy went on, "don't I seem foreign to you? Say, Swedish? Maybe I remind you of one of those girls you were talking about?"

Guzzler looked at Lucy, the silliness of their

conversation eluding him as well as her. "There was a German girl once. From Düsseldorf. She had sparkling eyes like yours. And she was warm, like you, and petite and . . . Well, she was very lovely."

Lucy moved an inch closer and lowered her voice. "Did you ever, you know—did you? You know," she whispered naughtily.

Guzzler leaned away and feigned surprise. "Why, Lucy! What a question! Of course, I won't answer!" he said as Lucy burst out laughing.

"You did, then!" she said, touching him on the shoulder and bringing their faces close.

Guzzler was about to kiss her on the spot, right out in the open. He had to break the spell.

"I have an idea! Let's get a couple horses and go riding!" he said brightly.

But Lucy just chuckled knowingly. "Sure," she said. "I know a beautiful spot deep in a ravine. It's very private."

Guzzler touched her face. Her skin was silken. And her eyes told him she was more than willing.

"Come on," he murmured. "Let's go."

They were walking across the patio when Pam stepped out of the house. Guzzler had his arm around Lucy's waist. That was the first thing Pam noticed.

"Hi," Lucy said nonchalantly.

"Pam!" Guzzler added in a brighter tone. "Hi there!"

Pam's voice was cool as she responded. "Hello, Lucy—Guzzler."

Guzzler was picking up a cold quality in Pam's voice. She seemed to almost hate him. Why? he wondered. Things could get pretty bad between him and Bobby if his wife didn't approve of his business partner, Guzzler thought. He had to take the bull by the horns and find out what was going on with her.

"Lucy, I just changed my mind. We'll go swimming. Why don't you go in the house and change while I have a word or two with your aunt here?"

"Okay." Lucy frowned. Maybe everybody at school was right about her. Maybe she was too fast with boys. If Guzzler really wanted her, she'd get him another time, she thought, as she stepped into the house.

"Pam," he said quietly.

"Sorry to interrupt another conquest," she said icily, "but we've had a lot of trouble around here with Lucy. We're trying to have her understand that sex is for grown-ups. And Lucy is *not* a grown-up. Not yet. In fact, she's a teenager with serious problems. So hands off."

Guzzler listened to Bobby's wife with a hurt look. "Pam. What's wrong?" he asked honestly. "Why do you dislike me so? Is it something I did?"

"You were going to take advantage of Lucy, weren't you? She probably threw herself at your feet, but that doesn't mean she can handle it, Guzzler. She can't!"

"We were going riding! And that's all!" Guzzler protested, embarrassed, guilty and angry all at once.

"Really?" Pam said sarcastically. "What is it about you? You think all women are for the taking?"

"I happen to enjoy the company of women very much, Pam. I enjoy them in and out of bed—and beyond that, I have made a lot of women happy. I think if you knew any of them, they'd be happy to tell you that," he responded in defense.

This man was appalling, Pam thought. "You know something, Guzzler, it must be very hard for you to be onstage all the time! Doesn't the curtain ever come down on your performance?"

Now Guzzler's eyes were searching her face with a look of confusion. "Why, Pam? Why do you dislike me? I asked you once, but I have to ask you again. This isn't about Lucy. You can't tell me it is. And it isn't about any other women I might have had either. But obviously, I have offended you in some way. And frankly, I'm sad and disappointed about that. I would like very much for things to be better between us. Can you understand that?"

He was telling the truth, Pam thought, suddenly embarrassed. He was right. She really was coming on like some sort of harpie! Had she actually been standing here having it out with Bobby's old friend, a man she hardly knew? Pam was horrified by her own behavior. Why? he was asking. Why? she had to ask herself now.

Pam sputtered a response. "I understand. Because I want things to be better between us, too. It's just that, well, I don't like what's happening to Bobby since you got here. He isn't thinking straight about things anymore. It's all

Guzzler this and Guzzler that. And the life he was working so hard to build for himself has just kind of been thrown away while you guys go out and play! Bobby has a lot to lose, Guzzler. He worked hard for what he had before you got here. He was moving toward some real independence and creativity, and now that you're here, it's like he's thrown up his hands because the circus has come to town! And I'm scared for him! Am I making any sense?"

Guzzler was listening intently. "Yes. Completely," he said seriously. "But there's also something you're leaving out, Pam. I know Bobby needs to be independent and I would never do anything I thought might jeopardize that independence 'cause I love Bobby. I do! Pam, I never had any brothers or sisters, and when I met Bobby, well, he was like an overgrown puppy who needed a friend. Somehow, I was the guy he picked. He looked up to me, Pam, and that made me feel important. But I always knew there was a responsibility in it, too. And I still do. I want what's best for Bobby just like you do!"

Guzzler was quiet now. And Pam looked at him, seeing him as if for the first time.

"When I first met you," she began after a moment, "I thought you were a very shallow person. But obviously, I had you wrong. I'm sorry."

"That's okay, Pam. And for my part, I'll try to mind my Ps and Qs. Friends?" he asked.

"Friends," she declared as they smiled quietly at one another.

* * *

Following his father's car out to the spot Bobby had chosen to build on, J.R. was aghast. The little expedition Jock and Bobby were leading him on was turning down the same old road he had turned down with Jeb Ames and Willie Joe Garr. Bobby's little nascent shopping center was smack dab in the middle of one of the richest oil fields in the South—Southfork Forty!

"Here we are, Daddy," Bobby said, affable as a tour guide, as the men climbed out of their cars. "This is Section Forty, from those elms over there, past that well you capped up, and across to the highway back that way. It's a lot of land. And it's a choice parcel. We figure the people moving into this area between Dallas and Fort Worth are going to need things—your basic goods and services. A food shop, a tailor, a couple clothing stores."

Jock looked around him, deep in thought.

"You remember, Bobby. This is the very section of land I wanted to drill on years ago. See that capped well? Your grandpa Southworth nearly skinned me alive when he found out I was planning to drill here, 'cause he hated all oil men to begin with! And here I was—got your mama to marry me and was about to start drilling on his land. Well, since I wanted to stay married to your mama, I capped the damned thing. But your grandpa got so fired up, he went and put it in his will—nobody was ever to drill here! I got the same clause in my will. Ain't that right, J.R.?" Jock called out to his eldest son.

"That's right, Daddy," J.R. echoed, dying inside but trying not to show it.

"I put that clause in because Grandpa South-worth was right. You shouldn't drill your own land. It's like fouling the nest. I see that now, though I didn't at the time."

Bobby hesitated. "Daddy, is that your way of telling me to find someplace else to build on?" he asked.

But before Jock could answer, J.R. spoke up. "That's right, Bobby. No need to go chopping up Southfork! If you want, I can even help you find another parcel—someplace better—for your shopping center. I can just put out a few phone calls and—"

"Hold your horses, J.R.," Jock said gruffly, interrupting his eldest son. "There's something else here. If Bobby actually went ahead and built this shopping center, that would remove any temptation anybody might have to drill this land after your mother and I are gone. There's a lot of oil under there, you know. And if anybody ever got a look at the geologicals, they'd think your mama and I were crazy for forbidding drilling here."

J.R. was growing more and more desperate. Once the ground was broken for a shopping center, Ames and Garr would be out of the Panhandle so fast he wouldn't know what hit him.

"But, Daddy, surely that's not necessary. Bobby and I are the heirs to this land. And we certainly respect your wishes about it. And Mama's," he said courteously.

Jock smiled at his eldest son. J.R. was an oil man through and through. And other people's wishes didn't count for grass where an oil man was concerned, Jock mused to himself, not when there's oil under the earth. That's why J.R. was a great oil man.

"Well, J.R.—the shopping center would just be a little extra guarantee. That's all. And aside from that, I think Bobby is right about this area. I've been watching the changes for a while and I think the whole thing is about to really take off now!"

J.R. pleaded his case in a stronger voice. "But, Daddy! Think about Mama! You know how she loves the land! You let Bobby build a bunch of stores here and the next thing you know, he'll start subdividing the land and we'll be looking at garden apartments and dry cleaners out the east windows of the house!"

Bobby couldn't help but smile, though inside he was annoyed. Why was his older brother so unsupportive of his every move? "J.R.! Cut it out! Nobody is talking about subdividing or anything! You're overreacting, J.R. Calm down!"

But J.R. just argued more forcefully. "You know how Daddy loves the ranch now! You can build a damned shopping center any old place! You don't have to mess up Southfork to do it!"

Jock looked weary all of a sudden. "That's enough, J.R.!" he ordered. Then he sighed and gazed out once again at the expanse of land before him.

"Bobby, I think your mama has got to be the one with the final word on this. It was her land before she met me, and I will respect her wishes whatever they may be. Come on now, boys. Let's go!" he said and the three Ewing men walked back to their cars.

Sue Ellen was adjusting her lipstick in the hall mirror when she heard J.R.'s car pull up. Somehow she was able to think much more kindly of her husband after a morning with Cliff Barnes. Cliff just brought out the best in her, and that best extended even to J.R.

"Hello, darlin'," she called out as he walked through the door, a grouchy look on his face. "How was your meeting this morning? You look tired."

J.R. only grunted in response. "My baby brother has had some harebrained schemes in the past, but this one takes the cake. He wants to build a shopping center out on Section Forty. Imagine that. A shopping center standing over three billion barrels of oil. Does that make sense?" he muttered more to himself than to his wife. "Tell Raoul to send me up a bourbon and branch. I'm going to lie down for a while. And don't bother me this afternoon. I have to think."

Sue Ellen smiled tensely. "Whatever you say, darlin'. See you at dinner, then." She was used to it.

As J.R. ascended the steps heavily, Pam was coming down to greet her husband. She had been wrong and she wanted him to know she knew it. She wanted to throw her arms around him and promise that they would never quarrel again. She wanted him to smile at her and hug her.

She was surprised when J.R. grabbed her arm on the steps. "Try to talk a little sense into your husband, will you, Pam? He's going off half-cocked! And he's going to break Mama's heart in the process!" he said to the confused Pam.

Just as the door to J.R.'s room slammed shut, the big downstairs door opened again and Bobby walked in.

"Bobby!" Pam called from the stairs, as she ran to greet him warmly. "I'm so sorry we quarreled."

Bobby stood tentatively. "I'm sorry, too, but—"

Before he could say a word, Pam put her arms around his chest. "Honey, I talked to Guzzler, and he's really not so bad. He loves you, honey. That's the main thing. And I'm not going to hold anything that happened that night he got you drunk against him anymore. I'm so sorry I was rude to him, honey. But we had a talk, and I think we understand each other now."

Bobby sighed and drew his wife closer. "Thank you, Pam. I knew you'd like him once you got to know him. He's a great guy under all that bravado."

Pam nuzzled her face against her husband's neck. "Well, I know it makes you happy for him to be here. And what makes you happy makes me happy, too."

Bobby drew back and looked into his wife's eyes. Pam was a jewel among women, he thought, as he took her tenderly in his arms and kissed her warmly on the lips.

* * *

Miss Ellie sat in the big leather chair in the den, looking as if she had just been told she had three days to live.

"Believe me, I was surprised when the place turned out to be that same section I wanted to drill on, Ellie," Jock was explaining. "But I do think that area is going to grow. There's all kinds of signs—new houses along the highway, they're paving across the road . . ."

Ellie was doing her best to listen without reacting. Obviously this shopping center project meant a great deal to Jock if he was coming to her about it. Still, to build on Southfork? To commercialize the land? What about her father's wishes?

"But is a shopping center really any different from an oil well?" she asked, her voice weak. "You know how my daddy felt about that kind of thing, Jock, and I would never want to go against his wishes, even if he isn't here any longer."

"Ellie," Jock said gently, placing his big leathered hand on her shoulder, "your daddy was against oil wells. He wasn't against change per se! He believed in improvement. If he didn't, we'd still be living in that little clapboard house, for godsake!"

"But that's different, Jock," Ellie protested. "That was a home we built."

"Well, Ellie, the way I see it, Bobby's on to a good idea with this shopping center. And it means a lot to him. That's what I'm thinking about," Jock said.

"You know," Ellie reflected, "sometimes I

think the men in this family are all too concerned with success and money."

- "Now, Ellie," Jock said, "money isn't what it's all about for Bobby, never has been, and I doubt it ever will be. But a young man has to have something of his own. Has to make something that the world can touch and feel and look at. I think that that's what Bobby is trying to do with this shopping center. I think that's why it means so much to him. And I can understand that. That's what he should be wanting at this point, and personally, I just hate to stand in his way."

Ellie was silent. Was she standing in Bobby's way if she refused to give him permission to build on Section Forty? she wondered. Because that was the last thing she would ever want to do!

Just then J.R. walked into the room.

"Mama—Daddy. You've been here almost an hour and I know how you like to have dinner on time—" he began.

But Jock interrupted him brusquely. "This decision is more important than dinner, J.R.! Dinner can wait!"

J.R. shuffled from one foot to another. Inside, he felt like jelly. He had to do something to stop this whole plan before it became a disaster for him and Ewing Oil. If he could only buy a little time, he would surely think of a way to foil the operation.

"Mama, I've been thinking," J.R. began, turning to his mother with a look of fond concern. "Maybe if you had a little more information it might help you make your decision. Now,

I can have a few people on our staff put together a whole packet for you with everything you need—demographics, potential risk, marketing analyses—the works. That way you'll be more informed when you have to decide."

Miss Ellie looked at her son gratefully. "Oh, J.R.—that's a very nice offer," she said. "But this isn't really a business decision. It's more of a family decision. Jock, I've made up my mind. Let Bobby have the land."

With that Jock walked over to his wife, helped her from the chair and put his arms around her. "Good girl, Ellie. I know that wasn't easy for you. But you wait. Bobby will build the most tasteful shopping mall you ever saw."

The two senior Ewings embraced warmly while J.R. looked on in horror.

Chapter Five

News travels fast in Dallas. The next morning, when J.R. stepped off the elevator into the reception area, his secretary, Louella, stopped him.

"Mr. Ames and Mr. Garr are waiting for you in your office, Mr. Ewing. I tried to get them to wait out here, but they refused. I'm sorry," she said with a worried look.

J.R. sighed. He had had a hunch on the way to the office that he might be seeing those two before the day was out. "It's okay, Louella. You did your best," J.R. answered before he stepped into his office.

J.R. walked to his desk without looking at his partners. He picked up a bunch of letters and began leafing through them casually, acting as if Jeb Ames and Willie Joe Garr were nothing more than two pieces of furniture.

The men shuffled, waiting for J.R. to say something. Only after a few minutes did he begin, and even then he hardly glanced at them over his mail.

"Well, well, you boys are certainly getting to be early risers. And on a Monday yet. I would think you'd be tucked in bed sleeping the weekend off," he remarked casually, referring to the kind of ladies they kept company with on Saturday nights.

"Cut the bull, J.R.," Jeb Ames demanded. "What the hell is this shopping center all about?"

"You came to see me so that we could talk about shopping centers?" J.R. asked sarcastically.

"When a shopping center is going to be built on top of our collateral, you can bet we're mighty concerned, J.R.!" Jeb continued. "Remember, that oil under Section Forty is the basis of every deal we ever made. But now that Bobby's planning to build there, I'm beginning to think that the Red File and all those clauses you showed us from your daddy's will are just fakes! Maybe nobody gave you the right to drill there now or ever!"

J.R. could feel his blood tingling. Ames and Garr were closer to the truth than he could bear. He had to throw them off balance with a counterattack. His voice was cold and hard. "Don't call me a liar, Jeb, or you might regret it!"

It was Willie Joe who tried to play the peacemaker now. "Wait a minute. Wait a minute. Jeb, J.R.—let's just stay nice and calm. Now, let's start at the beginning, without any rancor, okay? J.R.—if Bobby does build on the Red File land well, that makes a problem for us, don't it?

We could come up dry on the Panhandle and that would be that. So you can understand why Jeb's upset, can't you, J.R.? Wouldn't you be if the tables were turned?"

But J.R. just looked disgusted. "I don't understand cowardice, Willie, never have. The way I see it, you boys have no right to be upset about any of this! I have always protected your interests. Always! But you know something, if you come crashing in here like this anymore, I may not be so loyal in the future."

Jeb was not impressed. "You better stop that baby brother of yours, J.R. — 'cause if you don't, I will!" he said threateningly.

"What are you saying?" J.R. demanded angrily.

"You know what I'm saying and you know I would do it, too. So you better be your brother's keeper, J.R. That piece of Southfork belongs to you and me and Willie Joe. Bobby doesn't get to do what he wants there! Not without big trouble, he doesn't!"

J.R. stood up from behind his desk. Seemingly unruffled, he walked around to face Jeb Ames. Without a word, he took his fist and smashed it into Ames's face, knocking the man down.

"Don't you ever threaten my brother, Jeb! Or anybody else in the family! You hear? Because, if you ever do that again, you're going to be mighty damned sorry," J.R. warned angrily.

Ames slowly struggled to get up with his partner's help, a thin trickle of blood running down his chin and spotting his checkered suit lapel.

"Listen, you two dumb turkeys," J.R. continued, his patience worn thin. "Get back to your offices. And stop worrying, will you? I told you I'll take care of this and I will take care of it! That's all I have to say!"

But after they left, J.R. sunk into the chair behind his desk. Ames and Garr were just crazy enough to hurt somebody if they thought they had to.

The office phones were ringing in triple harmony the next morning. Guzzler and Bobby had begun to work actively on their project and they were using Bobby's office suite at Ewing Oil as their temporary headquarters.

"Good morning, Ewing and Bennett," Connie, Bobby's secretary, would say. "I'm sorry, Mr. Johnson, both Mr. Ewing and Mr. Bennett are in a meeting—excuse me, I have another call, please hold. Ewing and Bennett. No, Mr. Ewing is not available at the moment. Please hold and I'll take a message. Good morning, Ewing and Bennett. No, sir. Mr. Bennett is unavailable but if you would like to leave a message, hold on please. Good morning, Ewing and Bennett . . ."

On and on it went. Calls were pouring in from Chicago, New York, San Francisco and Philadelphia. It seemed like everyone in the United States wanted to find out about the shopping mall being planned for the land between Dallas and Fort Worth by the new Ewing and Bennett Construction Company.

J.R.'s secretary, Louella, almost felt guilty as

she watched Connie struggle with so many phone calls. Louella was catching up on paperwork while Connie was burning calories! Before he arrived at the office, J.R. had just had one call from a Mr. Marsh, who wouldn't identify the nature of his business and said he would call back later. That was unusually quiet for J.R.'s private line. It didn't make sense, Louella thought, especially since Bobby Ewing's phone line had been almost unused till now.

In Bobby's office, Guzzler and Bobby were at two separate desks, each overflowing with papers, trying to keep up with the calls that were coming in one after another.

Bobby's eyes had a look of concern that his voice did not betray as he spoke to his umpteenth caller. "Well, sir, we will be accepting competitive bids. . . . We've had a lot of interest and we may be filled in that category. . . . I'm not exactly sure. We've had to revise our plans considerably over the past week. . . . Yes, I can let you know when you could see a prospectus. . . . No, they're not available yet. But as soon as I have one, you'll have one. Thank you."

Bobby hung up and pressed the buzzer on his intercom. "Connie, hold any calls for a few minutes. I need to get my head together and give my voice a break! Oh, and could you bring in another pot of coffee?" he asked, as Guzzler continued talking on the guest phone.

"Yes, sir, this is Mr. Bennett speaking. It's a pleasure to speak to you, sir. . . . Well, we have inquiries from J.C. Penney, Nieman-Marcus and Lord and Taylor so far. . . . Yes, sir. I understand completely that you wouldn't want to miss out. . . . Your first branch outside the New York area? Well, that would certainly bring prestige to us, sir. . . . I'll send you the information as soon as I have it!"

As Guzzler spoke, his eyes were conducting a private play for Bobby, a play that read, "Wow! Listen to this! And this! And *this!*"

Finally he hung up the phone. "Whoopie! Bobby!" he shouted excitedly. "I'm telling you this is the biggest thing since sliced bread! They're standing in line to get into our center! That was the president of Bloomingdale's himself, little buddy! And he's worried that *we* won't want *him!* Whoopie!"

Guzzler was so excited that he didn't notice the look of consternation passing over Bobby's face.

"Guzzler," Bobby pleaded softly, "don't you think this whole thing is getting a little out of hand?"

But Guzzler didn't really hear his partner. His head was too filled with dollar signs and success.

"That little model really did the trick! Leave it to Ernie Miller. Two days and he comes up with an entire model complete with trees and little well-dressed shoppers strolling on the premise! That's what impressed them, Bobby, that and everything else."

"Guzzler! You're not listening!" Bobby said firmly. "You've been so busy selling this thing that we haven't had a chance to talk about what's really happening here!"

But Guzzler figured Bobby was just getting

his first case of nerves. Any project worth its salt made its creators nervous now and then. He'd deal with Bobby's anxiety later. Right now Ewing and Bennett had fifteen minutes to get to a meeting with the Board of Directors of I. Magnum.

"Just take it easy, Bobby," Guzzler offered. "We'll talk later. But now we have a meeting across town with the board of one of the classiest stores in the South! Let's go."

"Okay, Guzzler, but I really think we need to talk," Bobby said with a frown.

"Sure, little buddy. Sure thing! We'll talk —later!"

J.R.'s office had the quiet of a library. Except for Ames and Garr, J.R. had not had a visitor to his office in a week. He had purposely told Louella to clear his calendar. With a strong sense of priorities, he had only one goal right now—to clear up this little problem of Ewing and Bennett's shopping center.

Brooding at his desk day after day, the oil executive had made only one well-placed call, to a private investigator named Marsh. Now his single task was waiting for Marsh's return call. Hopefully what Marsh would have to say would make Guzzler Bennett old news around Dallas.

The call came at exactly 11:15. "Mr. Ewing," Louella politely said over the intercom, "your call is on line one."

J.R. sighed with relief. Marsh was his first line of defense. If he had nothing interesting to say, it was a whole new ball game. Instinctively, J.R. felt he would have more than enough against

Guzzler Bennett. The man was a fraud if J.R. had ever seen one.

"Mr. Marsh, thank you for getting back to me so quickly," he said, turning his leather chair so as to look down on the city of Dallas as he spoke. J.R. always believed in being kind and polite to private investigators, secretaries, small children and dogs.

"Well, Mr. Ewing, I would have liked to get back to you earlier, but this is the kind of case where one thing led to another."

"Good! Good!" J.R. said, smiling for the first time in days. "What have you got?"

"Well, Mr. Ewing, to begin with there's an active investigation going on right now in Montana involving a very complicated merger and probable swindle. After that, the gentleman in question moved on to New Orleans, where several thousand dollars that his partner invested was placed in phony certificates of deposit and . . ."

Marsh went on and on, his every word music to the eldest Ewing son. After a litany of transgressions—national and international—had been recited, J.R. asked the investigator to send documented proof and hung up the phone. Life was getting sweet again.

"Louella, is Bobby still gone from the office?"

"Yes, Mr. Ewing. I heard them say they would be out till after four," the secretary replied.

"Good, good. Could you please ring up South-fork and ask Mrs. Ewing if she could possibly meet me for lunch at L'Arc-en-Ciel Restaurant

on Atlantic Avenue? That's Pamela Ewing,
Louella, not my wife. Tell her it's urgent. And,
Louella, you needn't tell Connie about the call,
you hear?"

"Yes, sir," the secretary responded.

Given her history with J.R., Pam had to be
surprised when Louella called with the urgent
message that J.R. wanted to meet her at two
o'clock at one of Dallas's most exclusive and
charming French restaurants.

Since her marriage to Bobby, J.R. had been
little more than a thorn in Pam's side. He just
couldn't seem to adjust to the fact that Bobby
had chosen her, of all women, to marry.

For one thing, Pam was the daughter of
Digger Barnes, Jock Ewing's business partner in
the 1930s—a man who claimed loudly and often
that Jock had swindled him out of his rightful
share of the business. Also, she was the sister of
Cliff Barnes, J.R.'s most hated rival. Though the
fact that she was a Barnes seemed to mean
nothing to Bobby, it meant a great deal to his
oldest brother. J.R.'s hatred of anything
"Barnes" knew no bounds.

The maître d' led Pam to J.R. immediately. He
was obviously waiting for her, a look of friendly
concern on his face as she approached the table.

"Pamela," he said in a warmer tone than he
had ever used with her before, "thank you so
much for coming. I know it was on very short
notice."

Pam stiffly acknowledged his thanks and let
herself be seated across the table from her

brother-in-law. "Frankly, your invitation was quite a shock, J.R. Somehow, I never felt we would be meeting for lunch," she answered dryly.

Having lunch with J.R. would be like meditating with a rattlesnake, she had thought to herself. Anything could be expected from him, and knowing him as well as she did, she was prepared for the worst.

"Well, Pam," J.R. said warmly, "don't you think it's time that you and I put our differences aside? As far as I'm concerned, you are one of the family. Oh, I fought your coming in, I know you're aware of that, but hell, Pam, you fought back and you won, fair and square. I think we should just bury the hatchet."

Six months ago, Pam might have fallen for all this, she thought calmly as she sat looking at the man who had tried so hard to destroy her marriage. But now that she had been married almost a year, she had no illusions about her brother-in-law. Obviously he had some selfish motive for calling on her today, and the sooner they got to it, the sooner she could leave.

"J.R., please. Do me a favor. Spare the frills. Why did you ask me here today?"

J.R. sipped his bourbon and branch with a sly smile. "You always could see right through me, Pam, couldn't you?" he asked in order to flatter her.

She bit. "Like glass," she replied.

"Well, let's start at the beginning. You know I care for Bobby more than I care about almost anybody in the world, don't you?"

"To tell you the truth, J.R., I can't honestly say I do. I think you like to *think* you love him, but the way you've treated him, some of the things you've done to him—"

J.R. had to get her off this track fast. "Wait a minute, wait a minute," he said, leaning closer to her across the table. "Let's try to find a little common ground here, okay? *You* love Bobby. Will you agree to that?"

Pam was startled. Of course she loved Bobby. What did that have to do with this little private lunch? she wondered.

"And you would help him, in any way, if he were in trouble, wouldn't you?"

"Of course. But—"

"And if someone were taking advantage of Bobby, you would want to stop that person before there was any serious damage done, right? Wouldn't you?"

Pam was beginning to feel scared. "J.R., what are you leading up to? Who's trying to hurt Bobby?"

J.R. said nothing. He simply leaned back in his chair and reached into the inner pocket of his Brooks Brothers jacket. Taking out a thick sheaf of papers, he handed them to his puzzled sister-in-law without comment.

"Guzzler?" she said weakly after she had read a few lines.

J.R. nodded slowly and dramatically. "That's right, Pam. It's all there. The partner he swindled in New Orleans. The one he robbed in Montana—and those are just for starters. The authorities will be here for him any day now.

They just need a little time to unravel the legalities."

Pam was silent.

"He came looking for an easy mark, Pam. And he found one. Our Bobby."

Pam took a deep breath. The information on the papers she was holding was frightening. But suddenly she remembered where she was and, more important, who had given them to her.

"J.R., how can I believe this is all true? You could have had these papers typed by your secretary and made to look real by getting a notary public!"

But J.R. was not insulted. "If you feel that way, Pam, and frankly, I thought you might, then I urge you to hire your own investigator. In fact, I'll be happy to pay for it. Believe me, I'm as sorry about all this as anybody. But I think somebody's got to warn Bobby before he finds out the hard way."

"Well, why don't *you* tell Bobby since you're the one who is so sure Guzzler is a phony?" Pam challenged her brother-in-law.

"Pam, Pam—Bobby wouldn't listen to anything I had to say about Guzzler Bennett. Not if it wasn't flattering, at least. My brother just doesn't see straight when it comes to Guzzler."

For once Pam had to agree with J.R. She nodded sadly.

"Listen, Pam," J.R. continued, "you are the one who has got to stop this project before Bobby signs anything with him."

If the information was valid, J.R. was right, Pam thought. But how? How could she stop him? Bobby was his own man, especially when it came to Guzzler Bennett.

"I don't know if he would listen to me either about this, J.R. He and Guzzler go way back, you know."

J.R. smiled. "You're a smart girl, Pam. You'll think of a way to get to him."

Pam leaned back and looked at her brother-in-law. He still looked like an incredibly smug and insincere man.

"May I ask," she ventured, "what it is that *you* will get out of this?"

J.R. laughed innocently. "Me? Get something from this?" he teased. "Pam, does a brother have to 'get something' for helping his brother? Besides, does it really matter?"

Pamela smiled weakly at J.R.'s guile. "No, I suppose not," she said.

"Well, do try their desserts. Their glacé flambé is truly magnificent." He winked as the waiter approached.

But as J.R. gave his order, Pam wasn't smiling—not at all.

Raoul refreshed Bobby and Guzzler's drinks in the den as the two men pored over the plans for the shopping center. The model was massive, and on top of it several large blueprints were spread out.

"Guzzler," Bobby was saying in as friendly a tone as he could manage, "we've *got* to scale it down. It's too much! Much too much!"

But Guzzler Bennett only looked at his friend

with slight annoyance. "Keep your shirt on, Bobby! You're an equal partner here. If you think the thing is too big, we'll cut it down. No problem."

"Thanks," said Bobby with relief. "I mean, I really think our original plan was the best one. If we can stick to something like that, I think we'll be in good shape."

Guzzler looked up from the blueprint. "Okay, little buddy—let's say we knock out these two department stores. That'll leave only three. You know, I think the specialty stores will even be pleased about that."

Bobby shook his head in frustration and took another long swallow of brandy. "Guzzler! Guzzler! Wait a minute," he said suddenly, as if he had a sudden inspiration.

Rummaging through the stacks of papers, Bobby finally came up with a drawing of their original proposal.

"Here it is! Here it is!" he said, holding up the pitifully small drawing. "We have a supermarket, a dry cleaner, a drugstore and three other shops. That's it. Period. The whole thing fits in the area you now have designated for Bloomingdale's! Look here! I'm not kidding!"

Guzzler could hardly believe his friend was so bent on self-destruction. "Bobby, Bobby," he said in frustration. "When the universe is sending you this kind of prosperity, it just doesn't make sense to turn it down. Think big, Bobby! That's what this whole project is about! Getting you to think big! You've been put down so long by that jack-assed brother of yours that it's begun to affect you! A man doesn't win in this world unless he can think big, little buddy. That's the way the world works!"

But Bobby was unconvinced. "Guzz—please —the noise, the pollution, the amount of sewage and waste disposal—and remember, it'll all be right here on Southfork!"

Just then the door to the den opened and Miss Ellie appeared with a tray of coffee and a plate of chocolate-chip cookies.

"I thought you boys might be hungry. Will you be working all night?" she asked tentatively as her eyes drank in the model of the shopping mall on Jock's desk.

"That's not a model of the shopping center is it?" she asked, horrified, as Bobby looked down at his shoes.

But Guzzler just threw his head back and laughed with delight, oblivious to Miss Ellie's discomfort. "Yes, ma'am, Miss Ellie! It sure is. Here, let me get these things off the end of it so that you can really see it. You've got Bloomingdale's here, Saks here, and Lord and Taylor here. This one—we're not sure of. We've got a lot of competition for these spots, Miss Ellie. They're knocking down the doors to get into this mall!"

Ellie was stunned. The small group of stores her son had first talked about had now become a mall, complete with a multilevel garage and restaurants.

"There's even a small theater in this building

here, and a movie house along the west side here. Something for everyone!" Guzzler added with a flourish as he took a large blueprint and began rolling it up.

"I see," Miss Ellie murmured, the breath knocked out of her. She turned and quickly walked out of the room.

"Gosh, did I say something wrong?" Guzzler asked as Bobby glared at him.

But Bobby said nothing. He just quickly opened the door and followed his mother.

Instead of going directly to her bedroom, where she would have to face Jock, Ellie stepped out onto the patio so that she could sort through some of her disturbing feelings in the quiet night air.

Bobby had given his word that the shopping center would be a small group of stores, but the model she had seen in the den was of a huge complex. How could she rationalize giving her permission to such a plan? The spirit of her father seemed to hover over her, berating her for letting it all happen. And yet, her father was gone now. And Bobby was alive.

If Bobby was asserting his manhood on this project, wasn't that vitally important to his development as a human being? For so many years, Ewing Oil was the be-all and end-all of the men in the family, Ellie thought. And Jock and J.R. so dominated the company that it was hard for Bobby to find his place.

Still, it was Southfork. Southfork. The family home. Southfork, the land her granddaddy had purchased so many years ago. How could she stand by and let it be ruined by garages and stores and restaurants?

Just then the patio door opened and Bobby stepped out.

"Mama," he murmured, his voice full of pain as he put his arm around his troubled mother.

Miss Ellie had tears in her eyes when she turned to him, although she tried to be light. "Well, Bobby, it certainly has grown."

Bobby looked into her eyes and spoke seriously. "When people found out about it, Mama, the phones started ringing off the hook. It seemed like everyone in the world wanted a piece of the center. But tell me—how are you feeling about this?"

Miss Ellie sighed deeply. "I've got to be honest, Bobby. I'm overwhelmed. I feel like Southfork will never be the same once this comes. And that makes me sad."

Bobby turned his eyes away from his mother. "But wouldn't any development of any kind change Southfork? And besides, it's land that we never used, really. It's totally undeveloped, unused—just scrubland."

"Just scrubland. Never used. Bobby," she said, her eyes searching her son's face, "must everything be used? Isn't scrubland a home for the birds and the small prairie animals? Texas is their home, too, Bobby. And having empty land like that—it's somehow good for the soul. I treasure the moments that I ride by so-called scrubland. Oh, I know they say it's undevel-

Soaps & Serials™ Fans!

★ Order the *Soaps & Serials*™ books you have missed in this series.

★ Collect other *Soaps & Serials*™ series from their very beginnings.

★ Give *Soaps & Serials*™ series as gifts to other fans.

...see other side for ordering information

Soaps & Serials™
From Pioneer Communications Network, Inc.

You can now order previous titles of *Soaps & Serials*™ Books by mail!

Just complete the order form, detach, and send together with your check or money order payable to:

Soaps & Serials™
120 Brighton Road, Box 5201
Clifton, NJ 07015-5201

- - - - - - - - - - - - - - - - - - - -

Please <u>circle</u> the book #'s you wish to order:

The Young and The Restless	1	2	3	4	5	6	7
Days of Our Lives......	1	2	3	4	5	6	7
Guiding Light	1	2	3	4	5	6	7
Another World	1	2	3	4	5	6	7
As The World Turns	1	2	3	4	5	6	7
Dallas™................	1	2	3	4	5	6	7
Knots Landing™	1	2	3	4	5	6	7
Capitol™................	1	2	3	4	NOT AVAILABLE		

Each book is $2.50 ($3.50 in Canada).

Total number of books
circled _____ × price above = $ _____ .

Sales tax (CT and NY residents only) $ _____ .

Shipping and Handling $ _____ .95

Total payment enclosed $ _____ .
(check or money orders only)

Name _____

Address _____ Apt# _____

City _____

State _____ Zip _____

Telephone (____) _____
Area code

D 7

oped. But is developed land so much better, with its asphalt and concrete?"

Bobby was caught in a deep conflict now. How could he go against his mother's wishes in this matter? And how could he counter Guzzler, too?

"Mama—why did you agree to this in the first place if it makes you so unhappy?" he asked, without rancor. "I wouldn't have gone ahead with any of it if you hadn't said it was fine."

"I know, Bobby. And I appreciate your consideration," Miss Ellie said, looking up at her son's handsome face. "But there is something I love more than the natural terrain. And that is you."

Ellie reached up and kissed her son on the cheek. "You do what you have to do," she whispered, "and don't worry about me. I'm strong. I'll adjust. I just need a little time, that's all."

The woman pulled the '77 Chevy off the road, across from the long entrance to Southfork. It was late, pitch dark—the perfect time. The young man got out of the car and walked to the wide elm that stood directly across from the house, but about a half mile away. In his hands he carried a spade and a white business-sized envelope.

"Psssssst!" the woman called to him in a whisper. "Hey! You forgot the flashlight!"

The young man went back to the car and leaned through the window. "Shhhh! They can see a flashlight! There's still lights on in the house and somebody is still awake!" he said.

The woman sighed impatiently. "Will, they cannot see that far! Even Ewings don't have that good eyesight! Now take this flashlight so you can see what you're doing!" she insisted.

But the young man did not follow her orders. "There's enough light from the moon," he said, and began walking back to the tree.

As he pitched the spade into the earth directly in front of the tree, his eyes were riveted on the big white house.

Finally, the hole was wide enough and deep enough. Reaching into his pocket for a clear plastic bag, he put the envelope in, dropped the bag into the hole and began covering it over with dirt. When he was finished, he took a red poker chip, placed it over the spot and walked back to the car.

"Well, that's done." He sighed with relief as the woman leaned over and patted his thigh.

"Good work, honey," she said in a comforting tone. "See? There's nothing to be nervous about. Everything is going to go as smooth as glass. You'll see!"

Chapter Six

Pamela's eyes opened at the first streak of dawn as everyone else at Southfork slept. She looked over to her husband, who had struggled so hard to find sleep the night before. One restless nightmare after another had chased him until finally, only in the dead of night, his body had given way to dreamless sleep.

"Bobby?" she whispered, her voice featherlike and gentle, to his sleeping figure. But there was no response. Her husband was sleeping deeply and peacefully.

This was the time to do it, Pam thought with determination. The perfect time. J.R. had been right about Guzzler—accurate down to the last awful detail. She had had it all confirmed for her by an investigator of her own choosing.

Pam slowly and quietly slipped out of bed and pulled on her robe. She would confront Guzzler, honestly and forthrightly—tell him she knew the nasty game he was playing at her husband's expense, and tell him he wasn't going to get away with it this time!

Walking down the hall as silently as an Indian, Pam approached Guzzler's door and knocked lightly. There was no response. Her heart beating wildly with anger and fear, she turned the door knob and entered the room.

"Who is it?" Guzzler called out with fright. Then, seeing her, he sighed and smiled. "Oh, Pam. It's you! My God, girl, you scared me."

How could she begin? Pam wondered. How do you tell a man that you know he's a cheat and a fraud?

"I had to see you alone, Guzzler. That's why I came now," Pam said quietly.

"Oh?" he replied, raising an eyebrow licentiously. "And, uh—where's Bobby?" he asked.

"Sleeping."

"Oh, I see," he said, his eyes dancing over every inch of her. "Well, honey lamb, why don't you just come on and sit down and we'll, um, talk," he said, patting the bed near him invitingly. "In fact, you can just come under the covers and tell old Guzzler all about it while we snuggle up nice and warm. . . ."

A wave of nausea overwhelmed Pamela. How could this man think she would ever betray her husband? Especially for Guzzler Bennett!

"Guzzler, I'm not here for anything like that."

"Well, then forget it! It's too early in the morning for chitchat!" Guzzler said, trying to make a joke as he nestled into his pillow and turned over, feigning sleep.

Pamela took in a deep breath. The time had come to tell him everything.

"This is not chitchat, Guzzler. I'm here to talk about the authorities in Montana and why they're looking for you."

Suddenly Guzzler was awake, fully awake, as he stared at Bobby's wife with large gray eyes. She returned his stare with a hard look of her own.

Her conversation hit him hard. The very mention of Montana sent a chill through him. There had been problems up in Montana, big problems, and he had had to take some action he shouldn't have. But he had tried to stay within the bounds of the law—at least on paper. They could never really get him on anything, he thought as he had thought so many times since then, in order to comfort himself. Besides, Montana was ancient history! Who cared about things that happened a year or two ago? Only fools!

"My goodness, Pam. You sound so stern and judgmental," Guzzler said, regaining his equilibrium. "Can't a man make a mistake? 'Cause I made one in Montana. And I'm not proud of it, but I do fully admit it."

"Oh? And what about New Orleans, Guzzler? Was that the same mistake?"

Pam's accusation had the impact of a ten-ton truck. He was caught, Guzzler thought, panicking inside.

"Well, well, well. Aren't you a regular Nancy Drew!" Guzzler answered as coolly as he possibly could. "Did you actually go and hire a detective?" he asked.

Pam nodded, but she wasn't proud of the fact.

"Yes, Guzzler. Because I couldn't bear the idea that you might be taking advantage of Bobby and I had to know for sure. And I found out, all right. I found out you're a taker, Guzzler! You just think you can take whatever you want for yourself! Money, buildings, wives, friends, even reputations. You ran your daddy's business into the ground and then you traded on his good name to cheat people. And it finally caught up with you! But instead of facing yourself, and the truth, and making up for some of the grief you caused others, you went on the run and dreamed up the idea of coming to Dallas to see if that rich kid Bobby Ewing still looked up to you. He was a pushover, right, Guzzler?" Pam looked at her husband's friend sadly for a moment. "But the thing that really, really gets me is that you said you *loved* Bobby! What a rotten lie!"

"Listen, I've heard enough," Guzzler said, getting up and pulling on his robe. "You can call off the dogs. You win, Pamela. After all, you have right and might on your side!"

"No, Guzzler. This is not winning. Not knowing that my husband loses. Because he still has illusions about you! And this is going to hurt him real bad."

"Yes, it would, Pam. It would. And you know something else? You happen to be wrong about one thing. I do love Bobby. I do. His friendship has always been one of the most valuable assets in my life. You see, Pam, I was always the big man on campus. I had real dreams, and real ideals. I was going to be someone important, do something important. But after school, my father died and I got lost somehow. Everything I touched started turning to dust. I don't know why. I just . . . just burned out young. But Bobby knew me when I was still real, Pam. Maybe those are the wrong words, but God knows it's the truth. There was something in me then. Something good . . ."

Pam looked at her husband's friend with a mixture of compassion and contempt.

"I think what I'm trying to say is, do you have to tell him, Pam?" he asked, sounding wounded. "Is that absolutely necessary?"

Pam considered everything for a moment, but her mind and heart were at war as feelings of pity and sorrow for Guzzler flooded her. He was obviously in pain, too, and was trying hard to hide it.

"I don't know. I'm not sure, Guzzler," she said, as she turned and left the room to give him privacy to think.

When Pam walked back through the satin-wallpapered hall and turned into her bedroom, she saw from the door that Bobby was up. He was sitting at the window, looking out at the morning sun with a sad look on his face.

"It's a good thing I can trust you, Pam," he said, trying to hide his upset under a joke. "You know, Guzzler is what we used to call a 'skirt chaser.' Now, would you like to let me know what's going on between the two of you?"

Pam hesitated. What she was about to tell him was hard, very hard. But he had to know. For his own sake, he had to!

"Bobby, there are some things you should know about Guzzler, honey, before you get involved any deeper."

Bobby looked straight at her. "Are you talking about the Montana deal or the New Orleans one?" he asked.

Pam was surprised. "You know?"

"Of course I know, Pam. I wouldn't go into business with someone—not even my best friend—without checking things like that out."

"But I don't get it!" Pam responded, genuinely confused about her husband's motives. "If you knew he's so shady, why would you ever get involved with him?"

"Honey," he said, moving closer to her, "Guzzler is not shady, not really. He's just lost, somehow, and he needs a little help right now, that's all. He's a good man, fundamentally, and he got in trouble. All he needs is a way back. That's what I was offering him. That's all. 'Cause he's worth it, Pam. I know. See, you only met the man he is, I knew the man he was. And that man is worth saving, Pam."

Pam looked at her husband as tears filled her eyes. "Oh, Bobby. I think I hurt him. I think I hurt him bad."

But Bobby walked to her and took her in his arms. "It's all right. I should have told you."

Pam closed her eyes and shook her head. "No, I was wrong to interfere, Bobby. Very wrong."

Bobby drew his wife close. "Pammie—you were doing what you thought was best for me and I appreciate that. Very, very much. Besides, I'm going to have to hurt Guzzler myself. I was up half the night thinking about our shopping center, Pam, and I've decided to cancel the entire project. It was getting out of hand. I only hope he won't take it too badly. I know his heart was set on it. Is he still in his room?" Bobby asked.

"I don't know," Pam answered as Bobby dressed quickly.

"Well, I'm going to find him right now," Bobby said. "It's only fair to him for me to level with him right away."

Outside on the patio, Guzzler was adjusting his tie as he waited for the taxi he had called from his room. He would leave quietly, he thought, so that no one would see him slip away. It would be incredibly horrible if Bobby found out about everything. And if Pam had already spoken up, Guzzler certainly didn't want to be there when Bobby learned his idol was made of dust. It would all be too painful.

"Guzzler!" Bobby called, surprising him as he stood on the patio. "Good morning!"

"Bobby!" Guzzler greeted as if they had just run into one another on a crowded train. If Bobby didn't know, he sure as hell wasn't going to be the one to tell him!

"You're up early, as usual," Bobby said casually.

"'Il Allegro'!" Guzzler responded. "I love the morning! Always have. Remember when I'd get you out on the lawn at six-thirty for a morning workout?"

Bobby smiled fondly. Those early workouts

had been his first introduction to self-discipline. He would never forget them as long as he lived.

"Morning is when the dew is on the ground and the world is young!" Guzzler went on enthusiastically, as if he meant every word.

There was no kindness in delaying things, Bobby thought. He had to speak the truth, and do it now. "Guzzler, I've got to cancel the shopping mall. My mama is just too upset by it and I don't want to hurt her. The project is simply too big for Southfork, and it doesn't make sense to try to scale it down."

Guzzler nodded thoughtfully as if he were hearing this idea for the first time.

"Well, I agree completely, Bob. It's too big for Southfork. And it's your land. So you have the perfect right to decide about it."

"However," Bobby went on, "this doesn't mean I want to toss the idea of a mall away! I want to start working at once. We'll find another piece of land, and we'll build on it. And we can make it the most massive mall to hit the state of Texas!"

Guzzler breathed easier. He still had Bobby's respect. Pam had obviously not filled Bobby in on the bad deals he'd made before coming to Dallas. Now, at least, he could make his exit gracefully without shattering any of Bobby's illusions.

"Gosh, Bobby. I'd love to stay and scout some land, but I'm having some trouble in Caracas with the engineer and I've got to get there right away. They called me last night."

"Well, when you get back then," Bobby replied, with an edge of desperation. "We can go to work then."

Suddenly the sound of a car motor was heard and the two men looked down the long driveway of the estate to see a yellow taxi cab approaching.

"Look, Bobby. I won't be back. Not soon, anyway. After all, you made it without me all this time! You'll do great out there on your own. Just remember, little buddy, there's no substitute for confidence!"

The two men looked at each other, their thoughts unspoken, their affection undeniable.

"My cab," Guzzler said, the first to break the spell. "I'm flying to Venezuela this afternoon to see if I can straighten things out down there. Sorry to let you down, Bobby. But maybe next time," he said, getting into the cab.

"Guzzler! If you ever do come back, as far as I'm concerned Ewing and Bennett is a go! All the way!" Bobby said, helping his friend to the cab.

Guzzler looked at Bobby with affection. "Sure thing, little buddy."

"And here," Bobby said, handing a twenty-dollar bill to the driver, "this one's on me!"

"That's three cab rides I owe you for, Bobby!" Guzzler called out the window of the cab as it began to pull away.

Bobby waved as he watched the taxi grow smaller and smaller, and murmured quietly to himself, "That's okay, Guzz. I owe you a lot more."

Bobby turned to go back into the house, his shoulders slumped, his eyes sad. Then he saw Pamela leaning against the patio door.

The man and his wife didn't say a word. They didn't have to. They ran to each other and embraced, their sadness expressed by feelings, not words.

The slide projector cast a bright square of light on the wall, the only light in the darkened room.

"Would you get that damned coffee, Fay?" the older man asked gruffly. "I want to get through all of these again!"

"Oh, come on, Al! We're sick of seeing the Ewings and all their buildings and cars! Besides, we already know them like the back of our hand," the woman replied impatiently.

"You may, but your brother here hasn't gotten it all yet! Have you, Will?"

The younger man looked up from his place on the couch, then began rubbing his eyes.

"Wha' you say, Al?" he asked fuzzily.

"God damn!" Al yelled. "What the hell is it with you, anyway? You been sleeping while we're workin'? You know, since that last job, your brain has really gone soft, boy!"

This time Will struck back. "Now, listen, Al! We've been through these pictures a hundred times! It's six o'clock in the morning! You drag me out of bed at four and now you're complaining that I'm falling asleep!"

Al Parker snorted contemptuously. "Because I do things right, Will! That's why this time it's going to work so good that we never have to do this again! And this morning is the morning it's happening. So I don't care if you have to put toothpicks in your eyes. I'm running through them again and I want you to look at every one of them very carefully. Fay? Get over here!"

Will and Fay looked at each other in the dawn light, which was beginning to filter through at the edges of the dark curtains. Al was right and they both knew it.

"Okay, honey," she said, taking her place next to the card table set up with the projector.

A photograph of Southfork suddenly flashed onto the screen.

"Okay. One last time. This is the house," Al said authoritatively.

Next came a photo of Jock working out on the ranch.

"Will?" Al prompted.

"The old man. Jock Ewing," Will answered in a schoolboy monotone.

Next was a photo of Ellie, waving good-bye to someone from the patio.

"'Miss Ellie' Ewing, the old man's wife. Doesn't exactly dress up to her money, does she?" Fay commented cattily.

"Right," Al said, "the mother of our man, J.R. Now, who's this?"

Suddenly, J.R.'s face was spread thin on the wall.

"J.R. Ewing. That's J.R. Ewing."

"That's right, Will. Our boy J.R. President of Ewing Oil. And net worth: nine figures," Al emphasized.

"That means they won't hardly even *miss* five

million!" Fay joked, though her husband and her brother stayed serious.

Now a picture of J.R.'s silver-gray Mercedes was on the screen. Al continued talking as photographs came and went on the wall with a pulsing rhythm.

"He leaves his house like clockwork at eighten. That's a Mercedes 280sx. License plate —please note again: Ewing 3. This is his brother Bobby. Remember—he's taller than our boy and lankier, and he has darker hair. Usually leaves the same time, but not like clockwork. *His* wife: Pamela Ewing. No trouble there. And Sue Ellen Ewing, J.R.'s wife. No schedule whatever, comes and goes as she pleases—mostly shopping. Here we have Lucy Ewing—Jock's granddaughter—"

Al was interrupted by a long, loud wolf whistle. "Well, there's something to wake up for! Why don't we take her, Al?" Will asked with a goofy grin. "If she can put out I'll let her be my girlfriend."

"This is *not* a joking matter, you jerk!" Al exploded. "Now, we still have Ray Krebbs. He's the ranch foreman, probably carries a pistol and may serve as bodyguard from time to time. Here's the garage under the Ewing Building. And, last, J.R. walking into the building from the underground entrance."

Al snapped on the lights. "Now, this ain't going to be easy. Once he gets to Dallas, J.R. is free as a bird. He has a number of girlfriends, and all kinds of business deals. His schedule is scattered, so we're gonna have to live outside that garage and be ready to move on a dime."

"Well, that's okay. We'll just grab him like we did Gilhooley and Refelson. They weren't exactly easy to take, but we did it."

"Wait! We don't want another killing," Al stressed, looking sternly in Will Hart's direction.

"Okay, Al! Lay off!" Fay cried in an instant. "We're not going to have any trouble whatsoever. Right, Will? We're all going to stay cool and calm as cucumbers and do what we're told, *exactly*," she emphasized for her brother's benefit.

But Will wasn't listening. "J.R. Ewing. That's a great name, you know. J.R. Ewing. It even sounds like money," he said more to himself than his partners.

"Well, boys? Are you ready?" Fay asked like a singer addressing the band at a rehearsal. "'Cause if you are, here goes nothing!"

She laughed as she opened the door to the rented bungalow and walked to her car.

Lucy's face was screwed up in pain, her large blue eyes twisted with disappointment and sadness. "What do you mean, he's gone? Where did he go? And when?" she asked Bobby with desperation in her voice.

Bobby looked compassionately at his niece. "Sorry, Lucy. It's true. He took off this morning. He said he had some urgent business in Caracas, Venezuela, and he was gone!"

"Didn't he leave a message for me? Teresa,"

she pleaded, desperately turning to the maid as she served the family poached eggs on toasted muffins, "did Mister Bennett leave a message for me in his room?"

"No, Miss Ewing, I'm sorry," Teresa answered kindly.

"Now, Lucy—don't go getting your feathers all ruffled. Guzzler will be back sometime," Jock said matter-of-factly. "Now, pass me the home fries, would you, Ellie?"

"Bobby, you don't think he had any bad feelings about the shopping center, do you?" Ellie asked with a look of concern.

"No, Mama. He had business in Caracas. But he understood perfectly about the shopping center. In fact, he agreed that the project was too big for Southfork. He may even come back sometime to find another site, but right now —well, he's awfully tied up with his own projects."

Ellie smiled widely, her relief noticeable to anyone who knew what she had been going through lately.

"Well, in spite of the problem with the shopping center, I really liked having Guzzler around very much. When I was a girl, my mother and father were the host and hostess of all the cousins when they traveled through the area. I'd sit and listen as they told about other places and colorful people and all sorts of things in the world. I think that made me always look forward to having visitors even after I grew up."

"Well, Miss Ellie," Sue Ellen said with a pleasant smile, "we may have another guest in

Dallas real soon. I got a letter from my mother this morning, and she's thinking of coming to visit for a while with my baby sister, Kristin."

Jock muttered, briskly, "Where is it your mother lives, Sue Ellen? I always forget the name of that godforsaken place."

"Boca Raton, Florida," Sue Ellen replied politely, pretending to ignore her father-in-law's rude behavior.

"Well, it's a been a long time since you saw your mother," Ellie commented, trying to be warm, "but I imagine with the baby coming, she will want to be here more."

Ellie easily remembered Patricia Shepard. Though a grown woman, Patricia always seemed to be thinking about externals—things like clothes and "society" and who was "somebody" and who had what. To Miss Ellie, those were subjects more suitable for a teenager than for a mature woman. Privately, Ellie promised herself that on this visit she would once again try to find something to like in Sue Ellen's mother. Maybe she didn't know her well enough, hadn't yet discovered her good side.

J.R. said out loud what was on everybody's mind. "Sue Ellen, you will limit your mother's visit, won't you, darlin'? You just think of a nice polite way to cut her visit short. She can come again when the baby is born. That's six months away, anyhow."

Sue Ellen nodded. Her mother had been one of the strongest supporters of Sue Ellen's marrying J.R. Ewing. How ironic that her mother always fawned on J.R. and that J.R. hated her so, Sue Ellen thought.

Just then, Pamela dashed down the stairs, looking somewhat harried as Bobby followed, laughing. Together, they bumped into the furniture and murmured "Good morning" to everyone at the table as they stood at their places and gulped down some of their breakfast in a hurry.

"I'm late!" Pamela said as if to explain her behavior. Then Bobby, playing George Burns to her Gracie Allen, said, "One of us forgot to turn the alarm on. I wonder who?"

"I wonder, *too*, Bobby!" Pam teased before confiding in all the others, "He did!"

"She did!" her husband whispered dramatically, as the young couple hugged and nuzzled affectionately.

"Is that all you're having for breakfast, Pam?" Jock asked, giving his daughter-in-law a stern look, but one with a twinkle.

"I'll get something at work. I promise," Pam answered. "Bobby, I'm leaving."

"That makes two of us," J.R. said as he stood up. "See you at dinner, Mama—Daddy."

"Yes, have a good day, everyone!" Pam added.

"Well, wait a minute, you guys!" Bobby called out. "Wait for me!"

With that, the working members of the Ewing family were off and running.

In the driveway, J.R.'s silver-gray Mercedes, Bobby's red Mercedes, and Pam's beige Audi were lined up, one after another, ready to turn onto the road that took them from the quiet of Braddock into Dallas proper.

But this morning, unknown to them, they were being watched. Hidden behind the trees on the property across from the mansion, Al Parker stood still, his wristwatch in hand. It was eight-ten and everything was proceeding smoothly. He had dropped Will off at the airport at seven with instructions to borrow some nice, nondescript car from the airport lot. Will would get Fay and they would all meet again on the corner of Pacific and Harding—near, but not too near, the Ewing Building. Then they'd be ready to make their pickup.

Tonight they would have the privilege of being in the company of Mr. J.R. Ewing himself, President of Ewing Oil and the perfect golden goose. They'd be "socializing" while the Ewing family coughed up a little dough to get their old J.R. back. It was a beautiful plan.

J.R. lay against the warm satin sheets as he held the cool phone receiver in his hand. "Very good, Louella," he said into the phone, "that's why I called. I'll be back, oh, in about a half an hour." As he spoke, the woman beside him ruffled his hair and murmured into his ear.

"Darlin', I have to get back to work," he chuckled naughtily as he replaced the receiver, "but this certainly has been a satisfying and enjoyable lunch."

Now the woman sat halfway up in bed, the peach-colored sheet barely covering her.

"But, J.R., I never get to see you anymore," she protested, a hurt look in her eyes.

J.R. reached his arm out to comfort her. "You know, Judy, I miss you as much as you miss me, but I've been running my tail off lately."

Judy pursed her lips like a naughty school girl. "Well, I guess a little time with you, J.R., is better than a lot of time with somebody else. That's all I have to say."

Suddenly J.R.'s desire was greater than the pull of the office. Turning to the woman, he took her in his arms. "You just remember that, sweetheart," he said as she slithered down under the sheets.

The woman giggled as J.R. leaned over her.

"Well, I guess I can keep those turkeys waiting," he murmured before he buried his head in the crook of her neck.

Judy let out a low, sultry moan. "Oh, J.R. —you are a wonderful man!" she murmured.

"I know, darlin'. It's a shame other people don't see it that way. They're really missing out on a good thing!" He chuckled.

At the office, Bobby was in a panic. His architect on the Tuckahoe houses, Aaron Jones, had just called and told him to get out to the site immediately. The mill had just sent the final order of lumber and it had all been cut to the wrong specifications. Worse, the mill was claiming the shipment they had sent was exactly what had been ordered and had refused to exchange the material.

"Well, I'd better get out there right away,"

Bobby told Aaron over the phone. "Would you do me a favor and call Lou? Tell him I'm on my way."

"Will do, Bobby. Good luck."

Bobby walked to the closet, got his raincoat and hurried past his secretary's desk.

"Connie—I've got to get out to the site right away. If anybody calls, tell them I'll be back by three."

"Okay, Mr. Ewing," Connie replied.

Bobby got on the elevator and pressed G for the garage. He walked to his car, holding the key, but stopped short of the vehicle. From five feet away, he saw that the left tire was completely flat.

Retreating, he went to the elevator and reversed his steps.

Connie and Louella registered surprise to see him back so soon.

"Louella," Bobby asked in a slightly hassled tone, "is J.R. back yet? I have a flat tire."

"No, Mr. Ewing. He has people waiting for him, but he isn't back from his other meeting yet. He said he was on his way, but that was almost an hour ago."

"Well, I need to borrow his car. I've got to get out to the site right away. Do you have the spare set of keys?"

Louella reached into her desk and took out the keys to the silver-gray Mercedes. "Here they are, Mr. Ewing."

"Thanks, Louella. Oh, and call Johnny so that he can fix the tire later today. I need the car tonight. Tell J.R. I'll drive his car back to the ranch by dinnertime. He can take my car home. And tell him I'll be very careful—you know how he feels about people borrowing his car."

Louella laughed. Her boss's possessiveness of his automobiles was an office joke.

"Okay, Mr. Ewing. And drive carefully. J.R. claims there's curse on that car when somebody else is driving it," she joked.

"That's J.R.," Bobby replied with a smile.

Al Parker was standing across the street from the Ewing Building when he saw the silver-gray Mercedes coming out of the garage. He quickly pulled a walkie-talkie from his jacket pocket and began speaking into it.

"He's earlier than usual. He usually puts in a long day."

"Look, he's J.R. Ewing," Fay replied over the crackling wire, "he can do whatever he wants —after he gets away from us!"

Parker broke into a run as the Mercedes stopped at the corner waiting for a light. There, he saw the white Impala that Will and Fay had "borrowed" for the occasion. Jumping in just as the light changed, Parker ordered Fay to drive as inconspicuously as possible, and they began following the Mercedes as it drove outside the city limits.

"Where the hell is he going?" Parker asked. "The ranch is in the opposite direction."

"Maybe he has a girlfriend he's planning to visit," Will said.

"Yeah!" Fay added cheerfully. "Or maybe he's going to visit a farmer who found some oil in his backyard and doesn't know what to do with it!"

"Well, wherever he's going, it's going to be his last stop of the day." Will chuckled, feeling in his pocket for his .45 handgun.

Chapter Seven

Playing "chicken" behind the wheel of a moving vehicle in the middle of a deserted country road was not Bobby Ewing's idea of a good time. But the white Impala that kept edging closer and closer to J.R.'s Mercedes seemed to be challenging Bobby to just that. If the other driver wanted to get ahead of him so badly, Bobby thought with irritation, why didn't she just pass?

Bobby decelerated. He was not in competition with anybody, and so he thought it best to slow down and pull J.R.'s car over to the shoulder of the road. Maybe that would let her know in no uncertain terms that he didn't want to play. In fact, she was welcome to pass him. The sooner the better, he thought. Drivers like this woman were dangerous.

As Bobby's car slowed, the white car sped ahead of the silver-gray Mercedes, and Bobby turned his car onto the road once again. But suddenly, he had to slam on his brakes. The Impala had turned itself in a right angle across the road and was blocking his way.

"What the hell is wrong with these people?" Bobby said aloud in irritation as he sat and looked at the car in front of him. Maybe they were in some sort of trouble. He'd better get out and ask them what was going on.

Bobby reached for the handle of the car, but he didn't get very far. Before he could climb out, he was looking down the barrels of three differ-ent guns as two men and a woman, all in sunglasses and stocking caps, surrounded the Mercedes. Bobby froze. They weren't the ones in trouble! He was!

Al Parker was the first to approach the Mercedes, his pistol aimed straight at Bobby's head.

"Okay! Just stay where you are!" he shouted as he made his way to the car and flung the door open. "Oh, my God," the criminal ex-claimed as he peered inside and saw Bobby. "We got the wrong bird! This is the younger brother!"

"That's okay," Fay muttered. "He's still a Ewing! He'll do. Besides, he's cuter than that J.R."

Al shot her a mean look; he didn't like his wife making little comments like that, even in jest. Then, turning back to the Mercedes, he flipped the door of J.R.'s Mercedes open with unneces-sary force, reached in and dragged Bobby out by the shoulders.

"You just stay nice and calm and you won't get

hurt," Parker ordered, remembering that those were the same words he had once spoken to a man named Gilhooley.

Will Hart clasped a set of handcuffs around Bobby's wrists, smiling into his face as he did. "Well, hi there," he said in a friendly manner. "Here's a little metal to help keep you nice and calm."

Bobby said nothing. He was doing his best to express no emotion of any kind, though his heart was beating wildly in his chest. This was the kind of situation that called for a calm, self-possessed attitude, he thought. When thieves smell fear in a man, he thought, things get worse.

"Listen," Bobby began calmly, as the trio surrounded him and walked him away from the Mercedes. "If you want money, I have five hundred dollars on me. You can take it, and I give my word, I won't even report this incident to the police."

But the shorter man and the woman began laughing, as if Bobby had just told a very funny joke.

"Five hundred, eh?" the woman said in a mocking tone. "Say, that's some big bucks! That's a hundred and seventy-five bucks a piece! That'll get us all the way to Tulsa and back, right, Will?"

"But I have credit cards, too. They're worth far more," Bobby added. Why were they walking him to another car? Why didn't they just take his money and run?

Suddenly the older man clasped Bobby's

shoulder with a forceful thud. "Get in the car. We're leaving," he ordered gruffly, pointing to the white Impala with his pistol, and shoving Bobby along.

"Wait," the woman said. "Let me tape him up first."

Bobby felt her cool fingers pressing thick hospital tape over his eyes. Then, everything was dark as the team pushed a hat over his head, placed sunglasses on him and packed him into the middle of the back seat, the woman and the smaller man sitting on either side of him, their hard pistols shoved into his hips.

"Listen, buddy," the older man said from behind the wheel of the car as he took off his cap and started the engine of the Impala. "We don't want to hurt you, but since we're all going to be spending a little time together, just remember, you're as good to us dead as alive."

It wasn't really true, Parker thought, but it was the kind of warning that had to be issued. Ewing had to think he would be a dead man if he tried anything funny.

Nobody spoke as the car hummed along the roads and the car filled up with the dirty smell of cigarette smoke and cheap perfume. Then the car stopped and Bobby was shoved out of the white Impala into the '77 blue Chevy. The team was ready to make the journey back to their place so that they could really get the ball rolling.

Parker's bungalow was a condemned property located on the outskirts of the Dallas–Fort Worth Airport. In another couple of months, the house would be torn down so that the airport could be extended. Except for the occasional holdouts who vowed to go down with their homes, the buildings were vacant. Some of the houses served as temporary quarters for local drug addicts, who met in them to deal and indulge. On Parker's block, all the houses stood vacant except the one that Fay and Al and Will had decided to settle in temporarily.

The blue Chevy drove into a garage operated with an electronic door opener, and the motor stopped.

"Home, sweet home," Parker said ironically as the car door opened and Fay and Will guided Bobby out of the vehicle.

"Watch your step, sugar," the woman warned Bobby as they stepped into the garage.

Bobby just nodded dumbly. He was in a state of shock now and was just following orders until he could think of some way out of this nightmare.

The slide projector was still set up on the card table in the middle of the room when the Parkers brought Bobby home.

"Okay, folks—let's get our guest settled," Parker barked to Fay and Will.

With that, Bobby was shoved in the direction of a small room with a boarded-up window. The room had a bed and lamp and night table and not much space for anything more. Around the foot of the bed, there was a six-foot metal chain.

Will took it and rattled it as Al shoved Bobby down onto the bed.

Bobby snapped his head around. "Now, wait

a minute! That's not necessary. I'm not going anywhere."

But Will just smiled cruelly and continued shaking the chain.

"Keep your shirt on, Ewing!" Parker barked gruffly. "You'll have plenty of room to get around!"

Bobby sat on the bed, dazed, as Will chained his ankles to the old-fashioned metal bedpost.

"Look—you really don't have to chain me. I'd be crazy to try to escape. And I'm not crazy."

"That's right, sugar. Any funny moves would be crazy—suicidal, in fact," Fay added, as she tore the hospital tape from his eyes.

His eyes stinging, Bobby blinked as he looked around the room. It was shabby, with torn and yellowed flowered wallpaper. Will twisted the chains around the bed and locked them.

"Well, this way you won't even be tempted," Will said.

"Wallet," Parker ordered.

"A pleasure," Fay said, smiling as she reached into Bobby's back pocket and withdrew the wallet.

"I got it!" she announced, holding it up for her husband and brother to see.

"Okay. Let's go. Let's leave our guest alone for a while. We got work to do!" Parker said, turning to leave the room.

"Wait!" Bobby yelled. "What's going to happen to me?"

"Well, it's real simple, Ewing. We're either going to release you unharmed *or* we're going to shoot you dead! And it's up to your family which we do! Hope you've been a real good boy, now. Let's go!"

With that, all three kidnappers left the room as Bobby remained on the bed. Through the wall, Bobby could hear them talking.

"Here's the driver's license. I put it in the first envelope, right?" the woman asked.

"Right. And where's the damned newspaper? We need that for proof that he's still alive. Now, here's the camera," Al explained to one of his partners. "It's easy. You point and snap. Then, press here and wait for the picture to come out here. We'll take him by that wall, I guess."

"Okay. The paper's right over on that table," Will answered, opening a package of salted peanuts with his teeth.

"Al, honey, should I write Cliff Barnes's name right on the envelope?" Fay asked, just to be sure. Any little deviation from the plan, one little detail not right, and the team could be in some mighty hot water.

"That's right." Al Parker was especially pleased with the idea he had come up with of using Cliff Barnes as a go-between on this job. Cliff, as Bobby's brother-in-law, had perfect access to the Ewing family. And, he was known in Dallas as a certified liberal—easy on crime and hard on big oil. He wasn't going to want any bloodshed. Those types never did.

"Al," Will said, munching the nuts slowly and speaking with his mouth half full, "I don't know about using Cliff Barnes. If he's the guy's brother-in-law he may get crazy or something. I mean, if somebody messed with you, wouldn't I want to kill them?"

"Will, honey! Aren't you sweet!" Fay commented with delight.

But Parker wasn't up for any nonsense. "He ain't going to get crazy. He's a lawyer, a politician. He can't afford to get crazy," Parker replied simply.

"I don't know, Al, you never know. Maybe he won't do like he's told! He could get real crazy—"

Suddenly Parker exploded with anger. "The only one who ever got crazy around here was you! Our go-betweens have always been just fine! It was you didn't do what you were told and started shooting last time! And remember what we made on Gilhooley? Nothing! They don't pay for dead men, Will! That's what you've got to remember!" he yelled, as Bobby listened on the other side of the wall.

"So? So Gilhooley got killed! Big deal! The world loses another corporation chairman! What's the big deal!" Fay was yelling in competition with her husband to protect her brother. "Besides, that's all over. It's ancient history. Now, are we using Barnes or not? We haven't got all night here. Come on, Will. Barnes is a great idea. Let's stick with it."

"Okay," Will said, suddenly depressed as he fell into his chair with a vision of Gilhooley slumping to the ground in front of him. The man's blood had oozed onto the floor and bloodied up his shoes as his face turned blue. It had been sickening.

"Don't go to sleep on me now, Will! Go get Ewing. It's time to take his picture," Al snapped.

Will slowly stood up, his equilibrium damaged. "Let me take the picture this time," he said. That would give him something to do —something else to think about. He needed that. He needed it bad.

J.R. Ewing was not pleased.

"Where the hell is my car?" he demanded of Louella. "I came up through the garage and it wasn't there!"

"It's okay, Mr. Ewing. Your brother had to borrow it because his had a flat. He said he'd either be back soon or he'd meet you at the ranch for dinner. And he said not to worry, that he would be especially careful with your car."

"Well, I should hope so," J.R. said, calming down slightly now that he knew that the car hadn't been stolen. Still, he thought, it was as annoying as hell to think of Bobby—or anybody else for that matter—driving his car. J.R. had a very special, very personal relationship with that particular car. He was convinced there was a jinx on it for anybody else.

Louella continued giving her boss his morning messages. "And he said if he wasn't back, to use his car. Johnny already fixed the flat. Oh, and by the way, Mr. Ewing, your two-thirty appointment left. He said he would phone you tomorrow morning from the Panhandle. He seemed very happy about the operation there, by the way. He says they're on the verge of striking."

"Thank you, Louella," J.R. replied, once again self-composed as he strode into his office.

Just then, the phone on Connie's desk rang.

Connie seemed perplexed, and mumbled nothing more than yes and no before she hung up the phone with a worried look.

"Bobby hasn't gotten to the building site yet," she murmured just loud enough for Louella to hear her. "And it's been over an hour."

"That's funny," Louella remarked, not really thinking too much of it. The Ewings went where they wanted and did what they liked, and it wasn't for their employees to wonder about those things.

Cliff Barnes sat behind his desk, reveling in relaxed self-satisfaction as he flipped through a brand-new issue of the Sierra Club bulletin. Everything was going well. After he had announced his decision to run for State Congressman representing one of the Dallas districts, support and volunteers had started to flow in. At the moment, he was taking a break from work to leaf through the magazine, refreshing himself for the long night ahead, when he would be addressing a group of schoolteachers from the downtown area.

Just then, his intercom buzzed and Cliff casually picked up the phone.

"There's a man on the line who won't say who he is, Cliff," his secretary told her boss. "But he wants to talk to you right away. He says it's urgent."

Cliff immediately fantasized that the caller was a fabulously wealthy, anonymous donor —maybe somebody who secretly agreed with Cliff about the rape and pillage of Texas by the oil companies in the name of the economy.

Barnes, Cliff could hear the donor say as his secretary put the call through, *I can't say who I am exactly, but I'm offering you three million dollars to run your campaign. No strings attached. You're a fine candidate, Cliff. You're serious. You're dedicated. You're clear-minded. And the people of this state need you!*

"I'll take it," he answered, immediately pressing a button on his phone connecting him to the caller. "Barnes here," he said, attempting to sound serious and dedicated and clear-minded.

Al Parker was speaking from a small phone booth on the far end of Pacific Avenue. He turned his face away from the oncoming pedestrians and tried to appear casual and confident.

"Don't talk," he said in a barely audible tone. "We have Bobby Ewing. He's alive and he'll stay that way as long as everybody does like they're told."

"Wait!" Cliff exclaimed. "What do you mean you have Bobby? Is this a joke or something?"

Parker used his voice with authority this time.

"Did I say 'don't talk'? Just listen! We have Bobby Ewing and we are prepared to kill him if necessary. There are instructions buried under the tree across from the entrance to Southfork. They're under a red poker chip. Now, if you people do what they say, there won't be any trouble and your sister will have her hubby back real soon. No FBI, no police—none of that! Or Bobby bleeds! Got that?"

"Yes," Cliff murmured, "but what . . ."

Suddenly the line was dead, as the dull buzz of a dial tone filled the attorney's ear.

Bobby Ewing was in danger. That meant

Pamela was in danger, too. Cliff vowed to do exactly as the man had instructed him. He would do it fast, and he would do it efficiently, and he'd get Bobby back to Pam safely.

Lucy was in the living room as the Ewings gathered for cocktails. Her legs tucked comfortably under her, she leafed through a stack of college catalogues that she had brought down with her from her room.

"What do you think, Grandma?" she asked enthusiastically as she waved a brochure in front of Miss Ellie. "Isn't this campus pretty? Look at all the ivy on the walls, and that old clock tower. It's just like one of those old Doris Day pictures or something."

Miss Ellie shook her head and laughed. "I never thought I'd see the day when you would be interested in going on to college, Lucy."

Lucy smiled widely. "Guzzler has been a real inspiration to me, Gramma! You know, there's just so much to learn about in this world. So many things to study. And I think it's really important to go away to college. Maybe I'll go up north—to Holyoke or Vassar or someplace like that."

Jock smiled and sipped the grape juice he had as his cocktail ever since he'd had heart bypass surgery.

"If you ask me, the best schools are right here in Texas! There's no need for you to go traipsing all over the country to get an education. Remember, there's nothing wrong with the schools right here in the Lone Star State."

"I didn't say there was anything wrong with

them," his granddaughter said, obviously annoyed, "I only said I might want to go someplace else. There's a big world out there, you know—a lot bigger than Texas."

Just then Pam arrived, looking confused. Bobby had told her he would probably be home early tonight but he still hadn't arrived. That just wasn't like him. Before Guzzler had appeared at Southfork, Bobby had always been reliable and true to his word. Pam tried to dismiss her fear and worry, but somehow she couldn't shake the bad feelings. Finally, looking out the window, she noticed Bobby's car in the driveway.

"Where's Bobby?" she asked the rest of the family. "I see his car but I don't see him."

"Oh, I drove his car home," J.R. said. "He borrowed mine to go out to the site. Supposedly, anyway. That's what he told Connie."

"What do you mean—supposedly?" Pam asked.

"Oh, nothing really," J.R. replied, pleased to get a rise from his sister-in-law. "It's just that the builder called at four-thirty and said Bobby never made it there. Maybe Bobby is busy with some blonde," he added, making a tasteless joke that no one else found funny.

J.R. wondered for a moment whether Bobby did see other women. If he did, he had to hand it to his little brother; it never showed. But then, J.R. thought proudly in regard to himself, maybe hiding things like that was a family talent.

"I'm worried about him. This isn't normal," Pam said quietly. "I hope he didn't have an accident or anything like that!"

"Now, now, Pam," Ellie spoke up reassuringly, "if there had been an accident, we would surely know about it by now."

Just then the doorbell rang, and a wave of relief passed through Pam.

"That's probably him," Sue Ellen said, going to the door.

But when the large door swung open, it was Cliff Barnes who stood looking at her.

"Cliff," Sue Ellen exclaimed, embarrassed and shocked. "What are you doing here?"

J.R. knew Sue Ellen had had a lover, but he did not know who that lover was. If he ever found out that her lover, and possibly the father of her child, was Clifford Barnes, he would surely destroy her. She knew that and Barnes knew that. And that is why they vowed to keep their affair a secret from everybody they knew. Pam Ewing didn't even realize that Sue Ellen knew Cliff at all. As for J.R., he was light-years away from realizing who Sue Ellen's lover was.

"What's wrong?" Sue Ellen asked as Cliff stepped passed her.

"I have to see your father-in-law, Sue Ellen!"

They were in the living room now. The Ewings were as shocked to see Cliff Barnes standing before them as Cliff was to be there. After all, Cliff was the son of Digger, the man who habitually muddied Jock Ewing's name with accu-

sations from long ago. Not only that, but Cliff
himself had publicly gone after the Ewings in
a long personal vendetta, though he always
defended his actions with political attacks
on so-called big oil. There wasn't a man in
the world that J.R. or Jock hated worse than
Cliff Barnes, except maybe his father. And there
wasn't a man Cliff Barnes hated more than J.R.
Ewing, except maybe Jock Ewing, the man who
had used Digger and then cheated him out of a
small fortune.

"People, it falls to me to share some bad news
with you. I got a phone call," Cliff announced
simply. "Bobby has been kidnapped. The kidnappers have asked me to serve as the go-
between." Cliff looked straight at Pam now, then
drew her into the circle of his arms. "Pammie
—I'm so sorry," he said, his voice now quaking
with emotion.

J.R. looked at his enemy coldly. He didn't
believe a word that Barnes was saying. Bobby
didn't have any enemies—not from outside the
family, anyway.

"Quit fooling around, Barnes. What did you
really come for?" he asked angrily.

Cliff released his sister and faced J.R., out-
raged.

"Do you really think I would lie about something like this, you idiot?" he asked incredulously.

Just then the telephone rang. Ellie, who was
standing near it, answered quickly.

All their eyes were on her as she listened

intently and then mumbled into the phone, "Thank you for calling. That will be fine."

"That was Bobby's builder," she said, her calm voice covering her panic. "They found the car Bobby was driving abandoned near the housing site. He said one of the men will bring it by later."

Jock had been standing quietly listening to all of this. Now, with the mention of the abandoned car, Cliff's news was becoming all too real. Bobby, his favorite. Bobby, the fair-haired boy. Bobby—kidnapped. It didn't make sense. It couldn't make sense and yet . . .

"But why did they call you?" Jock wondered out loud, addressing Cliff.

"I don't know" was Barnes's sincere reply. "They told me there were instructions for us buried across the road from the ranch entrance. I checked it out on the way in and, sure enough, I found them."

Cliff handed a sealed envelope to Jock Ewing. It was his place as Bobby's father to open the instructions. Cliff had not tampered with them in any way.

Jock ripped open the envelope and quickly pulled out the note.

"We have captured J.R. Ewing," he began reading. Everyone's eyes darted for a minute to J.R., who stood reacting to a number of emotions, mainly relief.

"He is alive and well and we will not hurt him if you cooperate. By tomorrow at noon, have five million dollars ready in out-of-series bills. Cliff

Barnes is to act as go-between. We will contact you about what to do with the money. *No* police, *no* FBI! Your boy's life depends on *you*."

Pam looked at J.R., her hatred showing clearly. Why Bobby? she thought. Why? And the look of relief on J.R.'s face made it all the more awful.

As if in a trance, Ellie made her way to her eldest son. "J.R.! We'll get him back, right, J.R.? Won't we?" she asked pitifully.

J.R. looked blank for a minute and then nodded dumbly, putting his arm around his mother's shoulders.

Cliff, white with fear, again turned to his sister to embrace her.

"Oh, Cliff," Pam murmured, close to tears. "Cliff! Cliff! What should we do?"

Just then, J.R. released his mother and spoke with authority. Getting Bobby back was *his* task, not a stranger's!

"Listen, Pam. This is a family affair. We'll take care of everything. Don't worry about it, Barnes, we'll take care of things just fine. You can go home now," he said, dismissing Cliff.

"Wait a minute, J.R.!" Cliff retorted. "I don't like this whole thing any more than you do. And I don't like being here any more than you like me being here! But this is my sister's husband we're talking about and he's in danger! Now, they contacted *me* about this and I intend to follow instructions and do just what I'm told. I would personally feel responsible if anything happened to Bobby because I didn't do my job right. I'm not about to risk his life playing some macho game!"

"Don't worry about it, Barnes. We can handle this by ourselves. We'll do it our way!" J.R. answered just as strongly.

"No, J.R.!" Pamela shouted. "You will do exactly what my brother tells you to do! This is Bobby's life we're talking about—not an oil deal!"

J.R. looked nervously in the direction of his father.

"Daddy?" he asked, looking for support.

Jock hesitated for a moment as Ellie spoke up. "I agree with Pamela one hundred percent, Jock! We don't want to take any unnecessary risk where Bobby's life is concerned! I think we should give them whatever they want and be happy to do it," she said firmly.

Jock nodded thoughtfully. "You heard your mother, J.R. We'll play it their way—for the time being, at least."

J.R. backed down reluctantly, throwing Cliff a look of intense hatred.

"Listen, J.R.," Cliff implored, trying his hardest to be reasonable. "This one time, we're stuck together. Like it or not, you and I are going to have to play on the same team."

But J.R. said nothing in return. He only stared at Cliff with a look of bitter defeat.

Chapter Eight

Late into the night, J.R. Ewing had lain in his
bed unable to give himself over to sleep. He was
full of painful worry and a rare but very real
self-loathing. His baby brother Bobby had been
kidnapped. And worse, the kidnappers had gotten Bobby only by a mistake. It was him they
had really wanted. Would they strike again
soon? he wondered.

And worse, to think that he had actually stood
idly by as Cliff Barnes had come charging into
Southfork and started ordering the Ewing family
around about the best way to handle the situation!

Sue Ellen slept soundly, the deep sleep of
pregnancy protecting her from care while her
husband tossed and turned at her side. Only late
in the night had J.R. been able to fall into a
soothing dream. In his dream, Cliff Barnes was
shining his and Bobby's shoes at an all-night

paper stand downtown. When they had gotten up to leave, Bobby had put his arm around his older brother and said, "Next time we'll go to a professional." Laughing, they passed a newspaper that read, "FBI wins!"

The message was clear. Operating without the benefit of the local, state or federal police—no matter what the kidnappers' instructions—was insane. Even if they did get Bobby back, J.R. thought furiously, the perpetrators might never be brought to justice. J.R. was damned if he was going to pay five million dollars from the family coffers and then watch those lowlifes walk away scot-free! Oh, no—the authorities *had* to be called in. And, if *they* didn't get Bobby back, more drastic measures could be tried.

By morning, J.R.'s sense of self-respect and self-possession were fully restored. It was time for the Ewing family to reassert itself. And for J.R., that meant taking matters firmly in his own hands.

J.R. walked down the hall of the mansion and tapped on his parents' door. Ellie was already gone. She had not been able to sleep all night from fear and worry, Jock told his son as he stared numbly at the ceiling. There had been no comforting her. She was downstairs now, making coffee for herself and anybody else who might want it.

"I always dreaded something like this," Jock said in his gravelly voice as his eldest son stood before him in the large bedroom suite.

J.R. looked at his father and a wave of pity

went through him. His daddy looked a miserable
ten years older than he had the night before.

"Daddy," J.R. began, "I've been thinking. We
can't let Barnes handle this affair. It's too crazy.
We're letting Bobby down if we do that. Now, I
think our first line of defense should be to call in
the FBI. They're experienced in these kinds of
matters. They'll know how to help us. We can't
afford to be dealing with an amateur, not where
Bobby's life is concerned."

Jock leaned back onto his pillows with a
weary look. "I don't know, J.R.," he answered.
"You heard your mother last night. She thinks
we should play it straight and, for all I know, she
may be right."

"But, Daddy! You know how women are. You
can't count on Mama to be thinking straight at a
time like this. Naturally, she's upset. Now, I
think I should just go ahead and call the FBI.
I'm sure Mama won't mind when she finds out.
She just wants Bobby back home like we all do.
That's all."

Jock was staring straight ahead, listening
without responding.

"Daddy? What do you say?"

Jock shook his head as if trying to shake some
terrible thought out of his head.

"The only thing I know is that the money
means absolutely nothing, J.R. I'll give them
twice that, three times, to get my boy back."

"You ease your mind, Daddy. I'll get Bobby
back. Alive—I promise," J.R. said. And with
that, he turned and walked confidently back to
his bedroom.

It didn't matter if he woke Sue Ellen. He had to call right away and he had to call from a room where Pam wouldn't see him. J.R. had heard of an FBI agent, Chip Mahoney, for some time. Even those on the other side of the law respected the man.

J.R. arranged to meet Mahoney right away. Mahoney would drive to Southfork and then to the bank with J.R. It was perfect. The FBI would be there from the very beginning.

As Cliff stood in front of the bank waiting for J.R., his face fell when he saw J.R. walk over with a complete stranger. There was only one explanation for that. J.R. had gone against the instructions.

Now, J.R. brazenly introduced the men. "Cliff, I want you to meet Chip Mahoney of the FBI. He's going to be working along with us on this case so that we can get Bobby out of this mess and make sure the perpetrators don't go unpunished."

Cliff had only been able to shake his head. How could J.R. do something like this when his own brother's life was at stake? Could the man really be so inhuman?

Cliff muttered hello to Mahoney and walked ahead of the other two into the office of Tom Ferguson, who was already at work stacking the hundred-dollar bills into large piles and wrapping them with paper labels. Five million dollars was a lot of money; it weighed over fifty pounds and it was hard to fit it into one suitcase. But that is what the instructions called for and that's the way it would be done.

But Cliff couldn't remain silent. After a few minutes he politely asked J.R. to step into a corner of the room as the bank official and the FBI man continued stacking the bills.

"J.R., I can't believe you! I leave you alone for five minutes and you call in the FBI! That's just what the kidnappers said *not* to do," Cliff whispered vehemently.

J.R. shrugged. "Listen, Barnes, as far as I'm concerned, you are nothing more than an errand boy! You're not going to run this show anymore. This is a family matter and our family will take care of everything—without your help."

"A family matter, huh, J.R.? Well, maybe you're forgetting that Pamela is my sister! This is a family affair to me too, you know."

"I'm talking about Ewings—the Ewing family, Barnes. Your sister may have married in, but she'll never be a Ewing. Never. Now, I intend to get my baby brother home safe and sound. And that means I'm dealing with the FBI, not you!"

"J.R.! J.R.!" Cliff tried to appeal to him. "Listen. I talked to the kidnapper. He was very, very definite. He was serious. Don't get creative now. Not when Bobby's life is in danger. This isn't a time to take chances!"

"Don't worry about me, Barnes. Or Bobby. Bobby is my brother and I'll do all the thinking from now on. You're here only as a delivery boy."

Just then, Mr. Ferguson zipped the long suitcase shut. "Five million, gentlemen. It's ready," he announced. "If we had had one day we could have marked the money, but I'm afraid we won't be able to trace even a hundred of it," he said apologetically.

Mahoney looked at the bank officer. "That's why the Ewings were given so little time. Whoever planned this knows the way these things work," he commented.

J.R. reached for the suitcase, but Cliff stopped him. "Maybe you should let Mr. Mahoney carry that, J.R. I mean, he's supposed to be your chauffeur, right? And that does seem awfully heavy. It'll look more natural to have him carry it, won't it?"

Mahoney agreed immediately. "Mr. Barnes has a good point, Mr. Ewing. That's good thinking," he added. J.R. relinquished the suitcase reluctantly and walked to the door ahead of the others.

"Tom," he called out to the bank officer, "thank you."

"Anytime, J.R.," the officer answered. "Just get Bobby back home."

And with that the three stepped out into the morning sun and headed for J.R.'s Mercedes. Mahoney opened the trunk, put in the suitcase and then walked around to open the door for J.R. and Cliff.

Across the street, Will Hart paid for his coffee as the silver-gray Mercedes pulled away. He had watched every move through the glass window of the restaurant just like Al had told him to. Now, it was time to report.

* * *

Bobby was eating a fatty, cold stew as Fay sat on a folding chair beside the bed watching him, her pistol on her lap. He was wolfing the food. And no wonder, either. It was the first meal he had had in twenty-four hours. Parker had explained the kidnappers' logic. Rich people should go without food now and then. It was good for their character. Besides, hunger made a man weak. Parker didn't like his detainees too frisky.

But Fay hadn't been able to resist talking Al into giving their charge a portion. They didn't want him sick, did they? she had countered. And even Parker saw the sense to that argument. Still, he didn't like the way Fay's eyes lit up when she talked about the man they had kidnapped. She was too eager to stand up for him.

This Ewing was a handsome man, Fay thought as she watched Bobby eat. Even unshaved and unkempt, he possessed a certain air. He was distinguished, a gentleman. Best, he was young. Fay liked that. Most of the people they had picked up before had been paunchy old men. This baby was young and—interesting.

As she gathered his plate and spoon, Bobby heard Hart entering the hideout. He was calling for Al and Fay. Fay rose to leave, winking at Bobby on her way out. It was obvious she was attracted to him. It made Bobby's stomach turn, but maybe it could be useful.

"Wait!" Bobby said suddenly. "Listen, Fay. These chains are scraping my ankles. Can't I be unchained? I promise I won't try to leave."

Fay stared at Bobby in confusion. Maybe she could take off the chains. Just the way they were rattling every time the man moved was reason enough to get rid of them.

"Maybe," the woman muttered, looking at his strong arms and the way the lamplight illuminated them. "Maybe I can loosen them a little. I don't think Al would mind too much."

In the kitchen, Al sat with Will trying to get an accurate account of what had happened when the Ewing family had picked up the cash from the bank.

"There's nothing to tell! They were out by eleven and they were carrying a large suitcase," Will explained.

"How many of them?" Parker asked.

"Three. J.R. Ewing, Barnes and the other guy," Will answered.

"The other guy?" Parker asked incredulously. "What kind of description is that—'the other guy'? *Who?*"

"The chauffeur."

"The chauffeur?" Parker baited his partner. "Jerk! The Ewings don't have a chauffeur. They do their own driving in case you didn't notice when we were going over our plans! Was it Ray Krebbs?"

Will tried to think very, very hard. Ray Krebbs was the ranch foreman, that much he knew. He was a big guy, too.

"Yeah, I think so. About six-two? Nice build?"

Al Parker looked at his wife's brother with disgust. "Yeah," he muttered.

"Then it was Krebbs," Will said, definite this time.

But Parker didn't believe it. This third man, this so-called chauffeur, wasn't part of the original picture, and as far as Parker was concerned something was fishy.

Fay glanced up at the dusty clock on the soiled kitchen wall.

"It's past noon, kids. Time to call."

But Al wasn't ready. He needed time to let Will's account sink in. "They can wait," he answered gruffly. "It'll just make them more anxious, that's all."

J.R. had a bad feeling deep in the pit of his stomach. Chip Mahoney wasn't the man he had been cracked up to be. He was too slow, too cautious. Maybe the way to go was to get Ray Krebbs and some sharpshooters to come in and do the job for a fee. Maybe a kidnap was like business; the government wasn't always the best way to go.

Looking at his father, J.R. stated his case as clearly as he could, although he was operating on nothing more than sheer instinct.

"Daddy, you know we know people who are better trained than the police and the FBI put together. I'm talking about people like Jeb Osborne and Frank Zucco. We can make an arrangement with the kidnappers—meet them—and knock them off at the same time."

Jock Ewing shook his head and sat wearily behind the desk in his study.

"Bobby told me where to put that sculpture," he said, vacantly staring at the Remington on his shelf.

"Daddy," J.R. persisted, "we let Barnes handle this thing and we may never see Bobby again! And the FBI is going to handle things too carefully. You know how they like to let people get away with crime. I don't like that, Daddy! I don't like it a bit."

"You think I enjoy sitting around twiddling my thumbs when my boy is in trouble?" Jock exploded. "You think that sits well with me?" he boomed, suddenly on fire.

"Okay! I hear you, Daddy! Then let me do this my way. Let's have a Ewing in charge."

Jock was thoughtful for a moment.

"I want to go to your mother. See how she's holding up. But I'll have Ray Krebbs come see you. Talk it over with him."

The mantlepiece clock in the Ewing living room read one-fifteen. Pam, who had twisted a handkerchief around her hand until her fingers were white, kept looking down at the phone, which had a recorder attached, as if the phone could help her. Chip Mahoney sat on one of the sofas watching her.

Finally, Pam couldn't stand it anymore.

"They said twelve! Why don't they call? What does it mean? Maybe they've already killed Bobby," she cried in frustration and distress.

"It's standard strategy, Mrs. Ewing. They want you good and worried. But they'll call.

Don't worry." Mahoney's voice was cool and understanding.

Pam looked at the FBI man and then back at the phone. She was terrified. Ellie took her hand silently. There was nothing to do anymore but wait.

J.R. sat behind Jock's desk in the study and faced Ray Krebbs squarely. A few years ago, they had been drinking buddies, picking up girls and running around wild together. But time and experience had changed all that. And after J.R. had gone after Garnet McGee, the country singer Ray had hoped to marry, their friendship had died a sudden and violent death.

"Ray, we've got to forget our differences now. Bobby's in danger," J.R. began.

Ray nodded. "Just tell me what you want."

"Get some boys together, Ray. Some crack shots. You don't have to tell them anything. Not now. Just make sure they're available and lined up in case we need them. Okay?"

"What's the matter, J.R.? You don't want to part with your money?" the foreman asked bitterly.

J.R. looked hurt. "It's not that at all, Ray. Not a bit. I just want Bobby back and I want the people who took him to suffer. You understand?"

The door opened and Cliff Barnes stuck his head in.

"Oh, sorry," he said, surprised to find Ray and

J.R. together, talking. "I left my briefcase in here."

"That's okay," J.R. said amiably, "we're finished."

Cliff looked confused for a moment, but then shrugged and picked up his case. Something was up, he thought, but there was no way to figure it out if J.R. wanted it kept secret.

Cliff crossed through the hallway into the living room.

"Cliff?" He heard Sue Ellen call softly from the stairway.

Turning, he saw her. She was a resplendent woman, he thought, a radiant woman. Pregnancy flattered her too. She truly did have a glow. But he had to remember she was married to another man, a man who would love nothing better than to destroy him. A man who would surely destroy her too if he knew.

"Sue Ellen—are you all right?" he asked as she walked down the stairs toward him.

"Yes," she murmured and for one awful, terrible, wonderful moment he thought she might actually kiss him.

"No . . ." he pleaded softly. But she didn't respond. Instead she spoke in a businesslike tone now as she reached the bottom of the stairs.

"Oh, Mr. Barnes. Have they called?" she asked politely, as if Cliff were a stranger.

The reason for her behavior was apparent in a moment; J.R. was crossing through the hallway to the living room. He was frowning. It was unsettling to have Cliff Barnes running around

Southfork talking to his wife and whomever else he wanted to.

J.R. met his wife at the stairs and put his arm around her. "Sue Ellen," he said loudly enough for Barnes to hear. "I know your manners are impeccable, but there's really no need to be polite to everyone—especially not riffraff."

With that, he swept Sue Ellen into the living room to await the kidnappers' next communication as Cliff followed, full of anger and amusement.

Just as J.R. and Sue Ellen entered the living room, the phone rang, breaking the awful silence that filled the room. Jock answered as all eyes fell on him.

"Oh, no, Sarah," he murmured, "no, she can't make any meeting today. And please don't call back. She'll call you in good time. I don't know when . . . Ellie doesn't forget things, Sarah . . . but she's busy now and she can't talk," he said curtly before he hung up. Then, looking at his wife he muttered, "The Daughters of the Alamo are having a big meeting." Ellie nodded. Her world had stopped dead when they'd gotten the word about Bobby last night. Nothing mattered now but Bobby.

Ellie was seated near the entrance to the dining room. Looking at the mantlepiece clock, which read fifteen minutes after two, she muttered, "I suppose I should do something about lunch."

But no one responded.

Then the phone rang again, and this time Pamela leaped to answer it before anyone else could.

"Yes?" she asked breathlessly.

It was Parker. "Let me talk to Cliff Barnes."

"I want to talk to Bobby! Bobby Ewing! Where is he? I want to talk to him!" Pam demanded, her eyes brimming with tears.

But Cliff gently disentangled his weeping sister from the phone.

"Barnes here," he said as Pam shouted, "Make him put Bobby on! Make him, Cliff!"

Miss Ellie rose and went to her distraught daughter-in-law.

"Stop it, Pam," she said compassionately but firmly. "That's not helping."

Pam looked at her mother-in-law with lost and desperate eyes. Miss Ellie was right, she realized. Making an effort to control her emotions, she sat by Cliff as he listened to the kidnapper. The only sound in the room was the whirring of the FBI's tape recorder.

"Listen, Barnes. We know about the FBI," Parker said, bluffing. "I told you don't call the FBI or we'll have to kill your brother-in-law. Didn't you understand that?"

"What proof do we have that he's alive right now?" Cliff demanded.

"Don't worry. You'll get proof. Take the money and go to the city park. The proof you want is buried at the base of the war monument under a blue chip. You'll find the next instructions there, too."

"Let me talk to Bobby," Cliff demanded, afraid that the kidnapper would cut him off soon.

"Remember, Barnes, call in the FBI and he's a dead man!" These were Parker's final words.

With that, there was nothing but silence on the phone. Cliff replaced the receiver and looked at Mahoney, who was shaking his head helplessly.

"He wants you out," Cliff said simply to the FBI man. Then, turning to Jock and Ellie, Cliff added, "And I agree. He should go. It's not worth taking a chance."

Jock looked at J.R. and then nodded reluctantly.

"You'd better go, son," he said to Mahoney.

It was inevitable, the agent thought. All families feel this way when they're in the middle of an ordeal. Suddenly, even the strong arm of the government wasn't strong enough, not against a kidnapping.

"I'll keep in touch," he said graciously.

"What now?" Jock asked, looking at Cliff.

Cliff sighed. "Well, I think we should do what the man asks, Jock. I'll go pick up the instructions and maybe when I come back I'll have Bobby. But he wants to make sure I'm not being followed. So please—" Cliff turned to J.R.—"see to it that no one follows me."

"All right, Barnes," Jock said as J.R. burned with rage inside.

Pam turned to her brother and embraced him emotionally. "Please, Cliff! Don't let anything bad happen to him! Please!" She began sobbing as her brother took her in his arms and squeezed her.

"Pammie, I'll bring him back to you. I promise," he said levelly before he took one last look at the anxious Ewing family and walked out the door with an air of determination and courage.

Chapter Nine

The war monument in Dallas was an old-fashioned bronze statue from a war nobody really remembered anymore. It depicted a bearded rider, holding a flaming torch, on a horse.

The monument was set in a far corner of the city park and after the lunch hour, papers could be found strewn about its base. Cliff kicked aside some candy wrappers in the front of the monument and immediately his eye caught the blue poker chip Parker had told him about.

Turning to make sure he wasn't being watched, Cliff dropped the heavy suitcase of money he was carrying, knelt to the ground and took out the gardening tool he had brought to dig up the instructions. About four inches under the surface, he found a photograph of Bobby holding a recent newspaper, a letter addressed to Pamela and a pawn ticket, all wrapped in plastic.

Grabbing the packet, he stuffed the plastic bag with everything but the ticket into his coat pocket, picked up the money and hurried to his car. No one seemed to be following him.

The pawn shop was on Norton Street. Cliff handed the manager the pawn ticket wordlessly, and waited. From the back room, the man returned with a fine leather wallet. It was Bobby's wallet; Cliff recognized the finely tooled Burgundy-colored leather immediately. It had been a gift from Pamela. But it was empty except for a slip of paper bearing a typed note that read "204 Norton St. Third Step."

The address was a long walk from the pawnshop, made all the longer by the heavy suitcase. But Cliff thought it best to leave his car for a while and proceed on foot.

Walking along Norton Street, Cliff watched the neighborhood change from middle class to no class. Finally, he found a ramshackle building bearing the numbers he had been looking for. The third step was empty.

Cliff knelt down to inspect it more closely. What if somebody, a kid or something, had picked up the message he was supposed to find! What could he do? Every second that ticked by could mean that Bobby's life was in greater and greater danger and now he had run smack into a dead end.

Cliff decided to sit on the step and wait. Maybe someone would contact him there. Maybe he would get a new idea.

But when he sat down, the plank beneath him gave way. It was badly broken. A surge of hope ran through Cliff as he lifted the step and found a mailbox key with the typed message "609 Ince Street."

Laughing in spite of himself, Cliff continued on foot. He had had a lot of clients who lived in this neighborhood when he was a young attorney starting out as a public defender, but never did he imagine he'd be walking along the street holding five million dollars in cash!

The apartment house at 609 Ince Street had been long deserted. There were still some readable names on the mailboxes, but not many. Frantically, Cliff tried the key in every one of the boxes, beginning systematically at the upper right-hand corner and working his way down. After a score of false starts, the key turned and opened the mailbox for apartment twenty-four. But it was empty. He tried the other boxes. No luck.

Cliff tried pulling the mailbox for apartment twenty-four out of the wall. Nothing was behind it but mildewed bricks. He was at another dead end. Now what?

According to his watch, it was already five-thirty. What had happened? What had gone wrong?

Exhausted, Pam's brother trudged back to the front of the building and nervously looked out along the street. There was nothing but a few parked cars. A Dodge Dart, a Plymouth Scamp, an old Volkswagon, a Chevy—all apparently with no drivers.

His spirits deflated, Cliff made his way back to his car and drove back out to Southfork. He felt like he had let Pam down in a big way, but what could he have done? Obviously the FBI had scared off the kidnappers and they were going to make the Ewings do some fancy dancing before they released Bobby—*if* they ever released him at all.

It was J.R. who opened the door when the weary attorney rang the bell.

"So, where the hell is Bobby, Barnes?" the Ewing demanded rudely when he saw Cliff was alone. "Or did you botch up like I knew you would?"

Cliff said nothing but just walked past J.R. to his sister and wrapped his arms around her. "He's alive. At least he was alive this morning, Pam," he murmured, fumbling inside his coat pocket for the packet.

The entire family was assembled now, waiting for Cliff to tell them what had happened. His arm still around Pam, Cliff turned to Miss Ellie. "I'm sorry, Mrs. Ewing. The last instructions led me to a dead end. There's nothing more I could do until I hear from them again. Oh," he added, reaching into his coat, "but there's a letter for you, Pam."

Pam eagerly took the letter and held it to her cheek for a moment as if she could feel Bobby's hand on it. Then she tore it open and read:

Darling Pamela—I am being treated fairly well and look forward to seeing you all again soon! Be strong now, Pam. And know that if there is a way back, I'll find it. Help my mother and tell her I love her. And

in case you need to, remember that my life
is complete because of you. All my love,
now and forever, Bobby.

Pam's eyes filled with tears as she handed the
letter to Miss Ellie and then took it back, folded
it and put it in the pocket of her blue silk dress.

"Barnes!" J.R. was suddenly shouting. "We've
had enough of your bungling! From now on, I'm
the man in charge here!"

His eyes cold and hard, Cliff looked over at his
enemy. The gall of the man, he thought. The
utter gall.

"Know something, J.R.? There's nothing I
would like more than to wash my hands of this
entire situation. You want to run the show? Fine
with me! I never wanted to be the go-between
and I never wanted to walk into this house. And
if it hadn't been for Bobby and Pam, I never
would have."

"Well, you can just walk out again and believe
me, Barnes, nobody will miss you."

"Great," Cliff answered, humiliated.

With that Cliff reached for the jacket he had
tossed over the sofa when he had first walked in.

"I've had enough of this jerk!" he muttered to
Pam. But before he could make it to the door, his
sister stopped him.

"Oh, no, you don't!" she shouted. Then, turning to J.R., she screamed, "What happened was
not Cliff's fault!"

"Oh, no?" her brother-in-law shot back, "The
man is too stupid to make a simple delivery!

Where's Bobby? He would be here now if your brother had any brains!"

"Listen, J.R.," Pam fired back, "the reason Bobby isn't with us now is because *you* called in the FBI! If anybody is to blame now, it's *you!*"

J.R. was shaking with fury now but he didn't want to display a bad temper in front of his parents. Looking at Pamela, he was consumed by the same special loathing he had felt for the girl since Bobby had had the lack of taste to bring her to Southfork.

Jock and Ellie were looking anxiously from Pam to J.R. This was not the time for division in the family.

"Okay, J.R. That's enough now. Cliff stays," Jock barked as his son's eyes burned with fury.

Will Hart was flushed with anger. Standing in the Parker kitchen, he leaned on the greasy countertop for support and tried to control his rage.

"Tell me again, Al. Just run it by me again! Because if you said what I think you said, you must be the stupidest ass in the entire world!"

"I'm telling you! For all I knew, there might have been an army of FBI men following him," Parker explained painfully as he looked over to his wife for support and understanding.

"But he had the money with him, Al! You told us he had the money! And there wasn't anybody else in sight! You told us that yourself!" Fay was screaming, as her brother silently cheered her on.

"Yeah, he did. He did," Parker muttered full of self-disgust.

"I mean, we could have been out of here by now!" Fay continued, rubbing it in. "And the funny thing is, you're always telling Will how stupid *he* is! Ain't that a kick in the head!"

"Okay, okay," Al muttered quietly.

"I'll call them now," Will suddenly said. "Yeah! They don't expect to hear from us tonight. It'll throw them off balance!"

This time it was Will whom Fay had to chide. "You know something, Will? Shooting Gilhooley used up all your brains!"

The vein in Hart's forehead was throbbing now and Parker knew he had to make things all right if the situation wasn't going to get out of hand.

"Listen. Listen, both of you. Now, we're all under a lot of pressure but let's not start attacking each other, okay? Here's what we're going to do. Tomorrow we call them and we arrange another drop. It's as simple as that."

"Simple, huh?" Fay mimicked. "And what if the place where we drop is crawling with the FBI?"

"It won't be. They weren't even there today. Today I choked. That's all." Parker was doing his best now to pull this operation together and sometimes coming clean was the best way. They were all tired, and they were all scared. He had to show them he was in control and that he knew the score.

But Will didn't seem to understand his partner's attempt to soothe him. His rage transformed to sheer terror, he sunk into a chair.

"I got a bad feeling about all this, Al. A real bad feeling. I never wanted to come to Texas in the first place. But you and Fay made it sound so easy. And after Gilhooley, I had to go somewhere. But they don't fool around here. One false move and we're dead, all three of us! They love that lethal injection here in this state!"

The kidnappers were silent for a moment as their partner's terror spread like an infection.

"We can't think that way," Parker said as gently as he could.

"But if we ex him out right now," Will went on frantically, "I mean—tonight—we would have a good ten-hour lead. We could be in New Mexico in a couple days! All we have to do is get rid of him. It'll be easy, too! I don't care anymore. Gilhooley was easy. And he never said a word after I plugged him up! It would take them months to even find the body. By that time, we'd be safe—and far away."

Will's eyes were shining. The thought of getting out—getting away, far away—was thrilling. "The money don't mean beans anyway! Let's save our asses!" he continued feverishly.

Al and Fay exchanged concerned looks. Will was going off again—way off.

"The money is why we're doing this, honey. Remember?" Fay whispered to him.

"And there's no sense in killing if we don't have to," Al went on gently. "Come on, Will, we can't think negatively now. You're just scared, and that's okay, as long as you don't do anything about it. Remember, we're going to get out of here. We'll be out of here by tomorrow night. You mark my words."

Bobby's ear was pressed to the wall; he had been able to hear every word as if he were in the room with them.

All day he had felt more and more confident that this gruesome situation would soon be over and he would be a free man again. His family was sure to cooperate with the kidnappers. And five million dollars wasn't such a large percentage of the family fortune.

But now Bobby was putting it all together as he listened. There were problems. Al had missed the pickup. Will was falling apart. Everything was changing, and rapidly, too.

For the first time, Bobby trembled. These people were crazy! What would it take to push them over the edge? The wrong look in his eye? And if he enraged them, how would they react? What if Will had a bad dream tonight? Maybe he would walk into the bedroom and shoot Bobby just to have it over. Just to see how the blood oozed out of a Ewing.

There was no other way. He had to get out of there! Whatever it took, he had to escape.

When Fay had loosened the shackles, he hadn't told her so, but they were loose enough to be removed. Quietly, covering the chains with the bedding, Bobby removed the shackles. He stood without a sound and made his way slowly and carefully to the window. Then, he felt along the edges. The kidnappers had boarded up the window with simple finishing nails, but they hadn't done a careful job. One of the boards was loose. If that one could be taken down, the others would be weakened. All he needed was to get three boards off. Three boards would do it.

In the other room, the kidnappers continued trying to reason with Will Hart.

"If we kill him, Will," Al said, "why would anybody ever believe us again?"

"Yeah?" Will retorted. "Well, I thought this was supposed to be our last job anyway!"

"Will, honey," his sister entreated, "how can this be our last job if we don't get the money! Besides, what happens if we run out of money a couple years down the road? You want to take a job pumping gas?"

Will was unconvinced. "I just have a feeling, that's all. I think we should ex the guy and get the hell out of Texas before dawn!" he shouted in frustration.

Bobby's fingers worked deftly with the metal part of his belt to pry the first board off the window sill. Finally he was able to lift one board, leaving a four-inch hole in the window cover. Not big enough to crawl through, he thought, but a start.

Now, if only the next one would come . . . Bobby was straining hard. The next board was nailed tightly. Still, if he pulled with all his strength . . .

Bobby yanked at the board with quiet force. The nail slipped out from the wall.

There was eight inches now. He was eight inches closer to freedom, to Pam, to the end of this ordeal. But as he yanked at the next board, the nail squeaked loudly, like chalk on a blackboard.

Within seconds the kidnappers were in the room, their pistols drawn.

"See!" Will was shouting. "He's just a slimy rat bastard and he doesn't deserve to live!"

For dramatic effect, Al held the pistol next to Bobby's temple. "You know something, Ewing, we were just talking about you and whether we should ex you out or not. Something like this kinda tips the scales against you."

There was nothing Bobby could say or do now. Closing his eyes, he waited for the shot. But before he knew it, he felt a thud in his chest and then a sting as he was shoved back onto the bed and the cool metal chains were tightened around him.

"Shackle him up tighter this time," Al muttered to Will and Fay. "Maybe we'll execute him in the morning, but right now I want to get a good night's sleep and I want you two to do the same."

After Will shackled Bobby to the bed, he turned and left wordlessly as Fay began to follow. She turned as she got to the door frame and looked at Bobby, her eyes full of admiration and longing. No one had ever tried to escape before. That took guts.

"Sweetie, that was mighty dumb of you," she said. "Mighty dumb. You know, these boys don't exactly fool around."

Bobby nodded, lost in his own feelings of despair.

"Still, I guess a man has to try," she remarked before she turned and left for the night.

Mighty dumb. Mighty dumb. How right they were, Bobby thought. Trying to escape was not only dumb, it was dangerous. One more provocation and Bobby Ewing would be nothing more than a name on a tombstone.

The Ewing family was in the living room again, though it was only seven-fifteen. Miss Ellie had asked Teresa to bring in a light buffet breakfast. But the family wasn't interested in food this morning. Pam sat with a plate on her lap, but had let the food go cold as she stared straight ahead. Sue Ellen, in the throes of morning sickness again, nibbled on a biscuit to settle her stomach. As for Jock, he didn't even attempt to eat. Standing at the mantle with a cup of coffee, he was lost in a sea of terrible thoughts and feelings.

Only J.R. sampled the french toast and scrambled eggs that were standing in the large silver servers with flames underneath. The food was delicious, he thought to himself, but he said nothing about it to his family.

His breakfast consumed, J.R. was ready to begin taking control of the situation. Here he was with a bunch of tired, rumpled people. What they needed was a little information, something to ease their minds.

"Mahoney did a check and they feel pretty sure that this is the same gang that kidnapped people in Vermont, Florida, Wyoming and Georgia," he began as his mother and father looked at him. "And they've released almost every one of their prisoners unharmed. Supposedly, they even treat their victims well while they're with them," he announced to the listless group.

Pam looked up, confused. "You said 'almost.' *Almost* everyone released. What the hell does that mean?"

J.R. felt everyone's eyes burning through him. He had only tried to give them a little information and now he had to tell them about Rob Gilhooley.

"Well, the last man they took they killed. He was Rob Gilhooley, President of Martex Textiles. But apparently he was a kind of a loud-mouth type of guy. Apparently, he practically asked for it."

"Oh?" Pam remarked bitterly. "Were you there? I mean, how do you know?"

"Well, I'm only telling you what the FBI surmised, Pamela. Perhaps I shouldn't have mentioned it."

A horrible silence fell on the room as the family members looked at J.R. and then down at the floor.

Just then the doorbell rang and Cliff Barnes entered.

"Good morning, everyone," he mumbled as he took a cup of steaming hot coffee. "Listen. I have a plan, an idea, and I'd like to check it out with you. Today, when they call, I think we should tell them no more running around. We'll ask for proof that Bobby's still alive—I'm sure he is, Pam, I feel it in my bones—then we level with them. We demand a straight and simple exchange, out in the open. The rest of the details they can make up. But we don't want any more goose chases. It's been too long already and it's time to get Bobby back!"

Jock nodded. He liked Barnes's plan, liked it a lot. The others agreed.

Even Miss Ellie smiled weakly. Cliff's plan was reasonable and if the kidnappers were at all reasonable, maybe she would have her son back by nightfall.

Bobby was finishing breakfast when Fay walked in to take his tray that morning.

"You were hungry," she commented as if she were a friendly waitress and he was one of her regulars.

Bobby smiled in spite of himself and nodded. "Where are Al and Will?" he asked. Somehow, the people who kidnapped him were taking on distinct personalities now. In a crazy kind of way he was beginning to miss them if he didn't hear them.

"They're out planting the next instructions," Fay answered.

"So—how much longer will I be here?" Bobby asked.

"Why?" she said sarcastically. "You gonna miss us when you're gone?" Moving to the bed to pick up the tray, Fay chided him. "That was mighty dumb, your trying to get away like that."

"Well, I thought I was going to be shot in the middle of the night. I heard you talking. Will wanted to kill me!"

"He did not!" Fay protested. "He was just blowing off steam. Besides, we wouldn't have allowed it. What do you think we are? Animals?"

Bobby lowered his eyes so she wouldn't see the affirmation in them.

"That's the thing that really gets me about you rich people! You think that other people are a bunch of animals or something!"

"Well, maybe that's what Mrs. Gilhooley thinks," Bobby said brazenly, looking her straight in the eye.

"She's probably on a world cruise now sobbing out her hard-luck tale to some other zillionaire! She's got everything she needs. She inherited plenty!"

"Is money the only thing that matters?" Bobby was sincerely trying to understand her. "Is that it, Fay? I don't think so."

"You don't think so because you don't know! You've got money. You don't know what it's like without it. Without money, you're nothing. Nothing!"

The idea came to Bobby in a flash of inspiration. Fay. Talking with her. The way she liked him. Being alone with her. It was simple.

"Fay, you want money," he said, "I have it. More than I need. Take me out now. We'll go to the bank. I'll see to it that you get so much that you never need more."

She looked at the kidnapped man with wonder

in her eyes. "What are you talking about?" she asked, intrigued.

"I'm talking about you and me, Fay, together. I could get you money. Lots of money."

Fay was perplexed. "You mean run out on my brother and Al?" She was suddenly tender.

Bobby was caught. That was exactly what he had meant. It was worth the chance. He smiled at her tentatively.

"Why not?" he said quietly.

Her dark eyebrows knitted together. "Just a minute. What kind of person do you think I am?" she replied with a nasty edge.

Bobby looked at her long and hard. He remembered the way she had taken his wallet, the smell of her cheap perfume, the tobacco stains on her teeth, the way she'd shouted, "So he was killed! So what?" What illusions did this woman have about herself, anyway?

"What kind of person are you? Well," he replied coolly, "I think you've given me a fair idea." She was a criminal, pure and simple.

Fay glared at him. How dare he talk to her that way! Was he so high and mighty? Raising her hand, she slapped it across his face so hard that her palm stung.

"You rich bastards are all alike," she muttered. "No respect."

Bobby reacted instinctively, as he would if anyone had slapped him. He grabbed her by the wrists—hard. Then, just as suddenly, he released her.

"Take it easy, Fay," Bobby murmured, trying

somehow to find a way to turn the situation around. "Let's calm down."

Just then, the door of the house opened, and Al called out, "Fay! Where are you?"

Humiliated, Fay turned to take another look at Bobby Ewing, her eyes burning with hatred.

"Ewing, I hate to tell you this, but you're a dead man. My brother was right about you," she muttered as she walked out of the room.

Chapter Ten

The Ewing family was trying to live life as usual. Before dinner, they gathered in the living room and Lucy played a simple song on the piano. At dinner, they complimented Miss Ellie's choice of menu without really tasting the food. After supper, they drank tea and coffee and adjourned to the living room for after-dinner brandies. It was a ritual they all knew well.

And Cliff Barnes, son of the hated Digger, was with them through it all. It was as if he were living at Southfork now, J.R. thought bitterly to himself. Watching Cliff as he spoke to Miss Ellie or Sue Ellen sickened the eldest Ewing son. Even Jock seemed to respect Cliff's judgment and seemed to consider his opinion in his own calculations. This was a situation, J.R. thought, that could not be tolerated much longer.

"Well, I guess we can all use some brandy tonight," J.R. said in an effort to be light.

Pam sank into a chair in the living room. She looked tired and wan.

"Cliff—how much more of this can I take?" she suddenly asked her brother, the pain in her eyes too intense to look at.

"Pammie," her brother answered reassuringly, "they're going to call, and they're going to call soon. A situation like this is just as important to them as it is to us."

J.R. was holding the tray of brandies now. Miss Ellie reached to take one, but the telephone rang and she spilled it onto the tray.

"I'll get it," Cliff said, breathing deeply before he picked up the receiver.

"Cliff Barnes?" the man wanted to know.

"Yes."

Al Parker was standing in the public phone booth on the corner of Pacific and First. The city was quiet now. Only a few people were walking through the business district, most of them young executives working their way up the corporate ladder and too tired by 8:15 to notice an average-looking man huddled in a phone booth.

"Is the FBI gone?" Parker asked.

"That's right," Cliff answered confidently.

"Well, great. Maybe we can do a little business then."

"I want to talk to Mr. Ewing," Barnes said firmly. "Before we do anything I want to know he's alive and well."

Parker chuckled nervously. "Sorry, Barnes. You'll just have to take my word for it. He's alive. Alive and well."

"So why don't you give us some proof?" Cliff

demanded vehemently. "You want five million dollars and for all we know you may have already murdered Bobby Ewing!"

Pam could hardly stand it as her brother continued. "Come on, now. You've got to be reasonable here. This is a lot of money."

There was a split second of silence before Parker's irritated voice was heard over the line. "Wrong, Barnes! I do *not* have to be reasonable! I don't have to do anything, because Bobby Ewing is with me!"

What more could he do? Cliff wondered. Nothing was worth aggravating the kidnapper further. "Okay, okay. I believe you. So, what's your plan now?" he asked coolly.

"Okay, first thing. Start where you were yesterday," Parker began.

But Cliff interrupted him. "No, no. No more wild chases. We're not interested in that spy movie stuff. This time, we want Bobby. We'll bring the money and you bring Bobby and we'll have a simple exchange."

Parker suddenly burst out laughing. "What do you take me for, a fool? Meet you and have the police and FBI there to greet me? No way, Jose!"

Barnes was sincere when he explained his reasoning to Parker. "I trust you that Bobby's alive and I tell you, you can trust us. We won't have anybody there because all we want is Bobby. We want him and we want him alive and that is all we want! Let's stop this pussyfooting around now. You want the money and we want Bobby. It's all very simple! We can meet somewhere out in the open. Nobody can cover us there and everything will be very short and sweet."

Parker hesitated. But the thought of getting everything over with was too good to let pass by. He thought of Will, the way he was getting crazy, and Fay and the way she looked at Ewing. The sooner this whole affair was over, the better.

"Okay," he said after a time. "Dawn. Near the power substation on the road to Denton. Turn on the gravel road south of the station."

The line went dead. Cliff recounted the call for the benefit of the Ewings.

"Denton. At sunrise. They'll bring Bobby. This time they're for real."

A sudden smile flashed on Pamela's face—her first smile since the whole ordeal had started.

"J.R., are you going somewhere?" Sue Ellen asked as she noticed her husband quietly walking out of the room.

"Well, there's not much good I can do here," he said politely, smiling slightly. "Seems to me that Barnes here has everything under control, so I might as well go where I can be useful. I have a few papers I left in the office that need attending to." J.R. nodded to his parents and the rest of the company and left.

A few moments later, Jock stood up and looked at the group. "Excuse me for a little while, folks," he said gently, "I think I'd better go lie down."

"Jock? Are you all right?" Miss Ellie called to her husband. Since his bypass operation, Jock was supposed to avoid stress.

"I'm fine, Ellie. Just a little tired, that's all," he answered convincingly. "I'll just be in my study, but please, don't anyone disturb me. I'll join you again in a little while."

The clock in the Parker kitchen read nine o'clock. Fay was thumbing through an old issue of *Glamour* magazine by the light of a flickering fluorescent light when Parker walked in.

"Hi, honey. How'd it go? Everything set?" she asked.

"All set."

Will Hart came in now from the living room.

"What's the plan, Al?" he asked.

"Tomorrow morning at dawn. We make an even exchange. Him for the money. Out at the Denton power station."

Hart looked at Parker with shock in his eyes.

"Are you crazy or something?"

"No. I'm not," Parker said evenly. "That area is wide open. There's no way anybody is going to surprise us. We'll get there early. Three A.M. That way we'll see them coming. Fay, bring him in here. I want to talk to him, and won't have the chance tomorrow," Parker added, nodding in the direction of Bobby's room.

"Send Will," Fay said coolly.

Will went to get Bobby as Fay and Al squeezed hands.

"This is it, honey. We're going to make it on this one." He smiled as he coughed with a smoker's hack.

Bobby was standing in the kitchen now, his eyes squinting against the lights. Since Fay had become disenchanted with him, he hadn't even been allowed to have his light on.

"Okay, boy," Parker began, "we're going to exchange you for a few dollars at dawn. Now, are we going to have any problems from your family? You'd better tell us right now. Because if they try and pull something funny, you are one dead man."

Bobby considered the question seriously before he answered. "My family would never jeopardize my rescue," he said calmly.

"Well, fella, I have a feeling you're right about that. So dawn it is."

"Maybe he's lying," Fay said to Parker.

"Use me as a shield," Bobby said coolly.

"Well, I'm not kidding. One false move from them and you're dead," Parker stressed.

"They won't try anything," Bobby said, meaning it.

The lights were burning at Ray Krebbs's cabin as ten cowboys sat around with shotguns on laps or next to their chairs listening to Jock Ewing.

"Boys, you better be out there by midnight. That way you can spread out and conceal yourselves. It's gonna be tough cause you won't be able to say a word for hours. You'll have to be real quiet. But J.R. will be right there with you."

"That's right," J.R. said. "And don't move till I give you the signal. The main thing we want is Bobby safe. And the money. And the kidnappers taken. In that order. Got it?"

"Okay," Ray replied. "You'd best get going now. You got a long night ahead," he added as he opened the door to let the cowboys out. Each man shook Jock's hand before they left as Jock wished them luck. Then it was Ray's turn.

"Ray! Bring him back!" Jock said. "But don't take any chances with my boy, you hear?"

When the fellows left, Jock looked at J.R. with a worried look. "I don't like operating like this, J.R. And if your brother gets hurt in any way, you know your mama will never forgive me. I wouldn't be able to forgive myself either!"

J.R. hoisted his shotgun onto his shoulder, then felt in his pocket for ammunition. "Daddy, I'm going to end this ordeal for you and Mama. You'll see. I'm bringin' Bobby home!"

Jock smiled sadly at his son.

"Your mother's going to wonder where I am. I'm going back to the house. God be with you, J.R. And no unnecessary risks, you hear?"

With that the patriarch turned and walked back to his house, his proud bearing crushed by the weight of fear.

It was almost five in the morning when Pam walked onto the mansion's big white porch in her robe. Just looking out over the big Texas prairie was somehow comforting to her.

Cliff was already there, waiting.

"Didn't you sleep?" Pam asked her brother.

"No. Did you?" he asked gently.

"No."

Pam sat on the old white wicker sofa.

"Oh, Cliff. I'm so scared. I love him so. And you, too, Cliff. The two of you are the world to me."

Pam looked at her brother in the faint first light of dawn. All the time that she had been with Bobby Ewing, Cliff had done nothing but criticize him and cut down the Ewing family. But now, she thought of all he had done for Bobby. Actions spoke louder than words.

"Your husband is a good man, Pam. I'm happy to help him," Cliff uttered quietly.

That admission meant more to Pam than Cliff could ever imagine. Deep inside, she sighed gratefully. Maybe everything would be good again—maybe even better than before. Maybe Cliff would get Bobby home and there would finally be peace between the Ewings and the Barneses.

The door opened and Jock appeared, struggling with the fifty-pound case of cash that he had kept in his bedroom all night.

"Let me help you," Cliff said to Jock, offering to carry the heavy burden.

Ellie came through the door now, too.

"Cliff," she said to the man who had served so well as a go-between in this dreadful affair, "I will be forever grateful to you if you bring my son home, where he belongs."

Cliff took a deep breath. *"If, if,"* he thought anxiously. But he made an effort to appear confident and strong. The Ewings didn't need to see his fear—only his courage—in this last awful moment before he met the kidnappers face to face.

Looking out over the flat landscape with the powerful binoculars he had purchased with the cash he had found on Bobby Ewing, Will Hart saw nothing but scrubland and the dawning

Texas sun. Everything was clear, he thought. Soon it would be over. And Al had been right, that bad feeling had been nothing but fear. Walkie-talkie in hand, he waited.

Just as the sun streaked out in a low horizontal line over the land, Cliff's car pulled onto the gravel road and drove to the designated spot.

Cliff got out of the car and sat on the fender. If they were going to shoot him, he told himself bravely, they would have to do it in the cold morning light.

Seeing Cliff's car, Will Hart sent the signal to the blue '77 Chevy carrying Al and Fay Parker and Bobby Ewing. Within moments, the Chevy pulled into the same gravel road, as Will made his way to it.

Cliff saw the car and breathed deeply with relief. Then, he leaned into the back seat of his car and took out the heavy leather suitcase as Parker's car stopped and the front door swung open.

"Barnes?" Parker shouted. "Is that you?"

"It's me," Cliff shouted back. "But where's Bobby?"

"He's here."

The back door of the Chevy swung open and Fay stepped out, followed by Bobby Ewing. Bobby's hands were tied in front of him. Parker moved quickly to stand behind Bobby, his pistol in hand.

Cliff looked at his brother-in-law as a surge of excitement ran through him.

"Bobby! How the hell are you!" he shouted.

Bobby smiled. "I'm good. I'm fine."

Cliff immediately started toward the trio, suitcase in hand, as Parker nudged Bobby forward. They all met in the middle of the road.

"You! I never thought I'd be so glad to lay my eyes on you!" Cliff gushed happily.

"You don't look half bad to me either!" Bobby retorted, smiling.

Parker nudged Bobby in the side with the pistol. "You two can throw your party later. We still got business here. First, I want to see that money. 'Cause if it's fake, this man is dead!"

Cliff smiled and reached down to open the suitcase. "It's not fake. Nothing to worry about. It's all there and it's all real," he said, picking up large wads to show to Parker.

Parker picked up the suitcase effortlessly in his free hand and swung it over to Will, who continued looking through it.

"Okay. Ewing—start walking," he ordered. "Then you, Barnes. I want separate targets in case anything goes wrong."

Bobby began walking slowly across the chasm to Cliff's car as the prairie was silent and the other men watched. When he was more than halfway to his car, Parker barked, "Okay, Barnes. You're next. Go!"

In an instant, J.R., who was hidden behind trees fifty yards behind the others, put down his binoculars and stood up with a cry. "Bobby's clear!" he shouted to the men who were crouched down in the prairie waiting for the signal. "Get them!"

With that a round of rifle fire volleyed through the air and Parker fell.

Bobby turned. The bullets were going straight toward Cliff, who was still close to the kidnappers! Without thinking, Bobby turned back and ran to his brother-in-law. He dove on top of him, knocking him away from the gunfire that was sailing through the air around them.

Cliff hit the ground, the weight of Bobby on top of him crushing his wrists into the hard, yellow earth.

Hart jumped into the fray from his hiding place. He began firing wildly in the direction of the unseen shooters. But within seconds, he too lay dead and Fay, in tears, slumped to the ground.

When the men fell, Ray, J.R. and the others came running up. "Bobby! Bobby! Are you okay?" J.R. shouted.

But before he could answer, Cliff had grabbed J.R. and was hurtling him to the ground. "You lousy bastard! You almost killed us!" he cried, beating his fists into J.R.'s chest.

J.R. was stunned. "These men are crack shots!" he explained. "They shoot to kill and they hit their mark!"

"Oh, yeah? Don't tell me that! There's nothing that you would like more than to get rid of me!"

Bobby looked from Cliff to J.R. Could Cliff be right? he wondered for one brief moment. But it couldn't be. J.R. was many things, but not a murderer. And his hatred of Barnes couldn't possibly go so far. Turning diplomatically to his brother-in-law, he said gently, "Look. We're safe and it's over. Let's not assume the worst, Cliff. Please."

"Now listen a minute, Bobby. And you, too, Barnes," J.R. asserted. "I promised my daddy I wouldn't take any unnecessary chances, and I didn't. Bobby, you were clear. Even you, Barnes!"

Ray Krebbs stood looking at J.R. in amazement. Cliff Barnes had been a good ten feet from being clear! The only reason the man hadn't had his head blown off was because of Bobby's quick response and sheer, blind, dumb luck. Ray opened his mouth to dispute J.R., but looking at the brothers and Cliff, and considering the ordeal they'd all been through, he decided to keep his peace.

"Come on," Bobby said finally. "I want to go home."

Turning and walking to Cliff's car, Bobby saw Fay being led away in handcuffs by a law official as Hart and Parker's blood soaked into the prairie.

Averting his eyes, Bobby sighed and shook his head as if to shake off the gruesome images around him. The nightmare was over. It was over—really over. And he was alive. Thanking God, and thinking of Pam, Bobby climbed into Cliff's car and breathed freely for the first time in days.

J.R. and Cliff followed silently. Their hatred had been escalated by the events of the morning. The stakes had been raised.

After a long and happy welcome home party, Pam and Bobby headed up the stairs, their arms wrapped around each other.

"I may never let you out of my sight again, Bobby," Pam said, sighing and holding on to his muscular body. "These past days took years off my life . . . because you are my life, sweetheart," she said, her eyes filling with tears of love.

Bobby embraced his wife and squeezed her hard. "I love you, Pam. And as far as I'm concerned, if I'm never out of your sight again, I'd be very happy!"

J.R. and Sue Ellen were coming out of the living room now. As Pam saw them over Bobby's shoulder, her face hardened.

"J.R.?" she said coldly. "According to the accounts I heard, my brother was almost killed by you and your men today!"

Sue Ellen looked startled for a moment, but quickly got control of herself.

"Killed?" J.R. said, almost jocularly. "Why, that boy has never been safer in his entire life!"

But Pam and Bobby ignored him now. They were on their way upstairs to spend a long happy night in each other's arms now that Bobby was home again.

Lying in the dimly lit bedroom, Sue Ellen scrutinized J.R.'s worry-free expression as he slept beside her. She had no illusions about her marriage. But she had made her choice: She would make the best of a bad situation. The love she couldn't get her husband to accept she would lavish on her child.

Sue Ellen felt a rush of triumph as she patted her slightly swollen abdomen. When her baby was born, Sue Ellen would have everything she wanted. But then again, that wasn't true. Invading her thoughts was the dream that she and Cliff Barnes would be able to raise that baby together.

As each day went by she convinced herself more and more that Cliff was the father of her baby. She longed to shout it aloud but dared not. It was a secret she had to keep to herself. Or did she really have to do that? Didn't Cliff have the right to know his own child?

But suppose she was wrong? There wasn't any way to be sure that J.R. didn't father this baby. She needed to talk to Cliff; she always needed him.

Sue Ellen shut her eyes but couldn't shut the image of Cliff Barnes from her mind's eye. She wasn't sure if it was the right thing, but she knew she had to see her beloved Cliff once more.